THE FOURTH SCROLL

THE SACRED FIRE SAGA
BOOK 2

KAREN GRUNST

HUNTER HOUSE
FICTION

To my husband
Together we've navigated the twists and turns of life

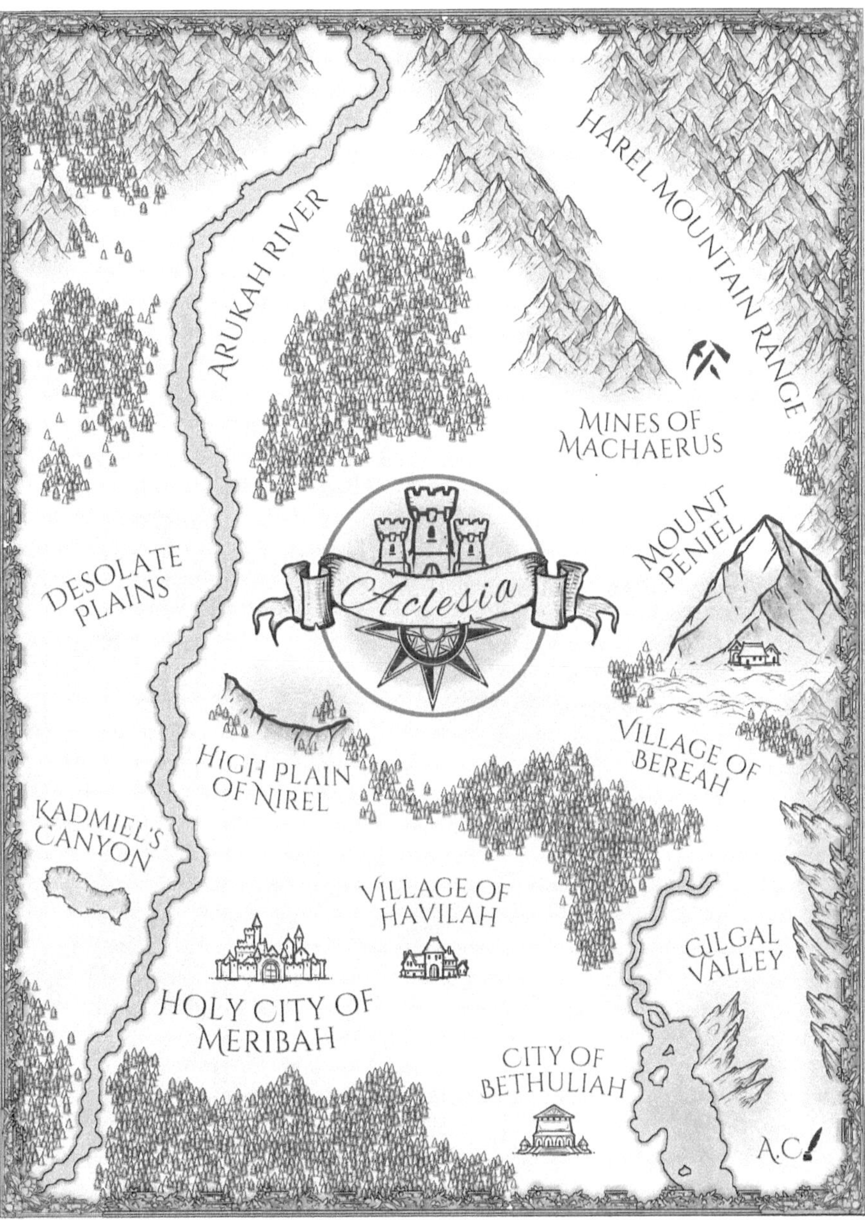

HAREL MOUNTAIN RANGE
ARUKAH RIVER
MINES OF MACHAERUS
Aclesia
MOUNT PENIEL
DESOLATE PLAINS
VILLAGE OF BEREAH
HIGH PLAIN OF NIREL
KADMIEL'S CANYON
VILLAGE OF HAVILAH
GILGAL VALLEY
HOLY CITY OF MERIBAH
CITY OF BETHULIAH
A.C

CONTENTS

1

THE BELL TOWER

In the bell tower high above the Square of the Patriarchs, the holy city appeared peaceful...but Sarah knew better. For she was blessed—or was it cursed?—to perceive the resentments, anger, and hatred of the city's residents.

But up here with her new husband, the chaotic swirl of emotions couldn't reach her. Even Ventus Furens, the cursed wind of the Desolate Plains, lay dormant on this perfect spring afternoon.

Sarah rested her head on Jacob's chest as they gazed out over the holy city. Her heart swelled when his brown eyes dropped to hers.

"So, where do you think we should live, Mrs. Eleazar?"

"Here would be my first choice." She looked down on the leaden roof of the cathedral, the dwelling place of the Sacred Fire. The one place in the holy city that always brought her peace.

But only the priests and their students were allowed to live on the grounds, at least until Jacob's older brother Peter took a wife. As the elder son, the south turret was his residence until he succeeded his father as High Priest of Aclesia.

"Trust me, we don't want to live in the south turret with Peter," Jacob said. "Not only is he unpleasant, but we'd have almost no privacy."

"No privacy would be a problem." She rose on her tip toes and planted a kiss on his waiting lips.

While she had no interest in sharing quarters with her brother-in-law, she was grateful to him for marrying them despite his obvious disdain for her. Besides, people knew her as a servant, a ruse concocted by her grandmother to hide her true identity. A more modest home would only be appropriate.

"Won't you miss this?" She gestured to the wide cobblestone promenade fronted by the elegant homes of the First Families that built the city over the centuries.

He shook his head. "We don't want to live in the Heights anyway...bunch of snobs."

"But this has been your home for your entire life."

He brushed a lock of hair off her face. "My home is wherever you are."

Sarah wrapped her arms around him. Wherever they made their new home, they'd be happy as long as they were together. Even if they could only afford one of the small houses jammed together near the western wall, where smokey haze hung thick above the chimneys.

That entire neighborhood could fit in most of the mansions along the promenade, especially the four-story marble monstrosity with all the balconies.

"Whose house is that on the end?"

But she knew the answer even before Jacob tightened his grip around her waist. "The House of Arcanus."

A shudder passed through Sarah as she peered over the stone edge of the bell tower. Sixteen years ago, Niccolus Arcanus had cursed her dying father with a Triatus curse. Anyone with the blood of Arcanus in their veins was honor bound to kill the children and grandchildren of Thaddeus Asher.

"Don't worry. We can't afford to live anywhere near them." A tremor of fear edged his voice.

According to her grandmother, it was vital that the Arcanus clan continue to believe Sarah and her younger brother Jonah were dead, buried with their parents in the Grove of Tears outside of the city. Only recently, she'd learned that Jacob's father, Matthias, had helped to smuggle Sarah and Jonah out of the holy city and away to the north when they were young children.

But did that mean Matthias's protection over her in the past would extend to the present? And how would her long-ago rescuer take the news that she and his son had secretly married while he was away?

Jacob's handsome face hardened as he looked down on the bustling square. A black coach approached the front of the cathedral. He pulled Sarah into the shadows with him as it came to a stop before the high double doors. A black-robed man with salt and pepper hair and a graying beard exited the carriage. He straightened the purple and white vestment around his neck.

High Priest Matthias had returned.

2
———

GOOD NEWS

Outside the door to the high priest's study, Jacob squared his shoulders and straightened his robe. As much as he dreaded this conversation, it was better to have it here than in the Great Hall where the scolding he was about to receive would be overheard by the other priests and students at supper. And at least he wouldn't be facing his father alone.

"You look like a man going to his execution." His older brother Peter smirked.

"I'm glad you're enjoying this."

"And we're just getting started." Peter laid a hand on his shoulder, then gave him a firm shove.

Jacob stumbled into the high priest's study.

Their father looked up from his desk. "Boys, come in."

"Welcome back," Peter said as he came to greet them.

"You're looking well, Father." Jacob ran his sweaty palm down his robe before shaking his father's outstretched hand.

"Yes, the hot springs do wonders for both body and soul. I feel thoroughly refreshed."

"That's terrific." Peter leaned against the mantel. "I sure hope it lasts."

Their father gestured toward the curving stone staircase to his private sitting area above. "We should eat before our dinner grows cold."

Jacob plodded up the stairs after his father and brother who chatted about the latest news of the city. He paused before the window overlooking the gardens. Through the tall oaks, he glimpsed the slate roof of the bakery where Sarah lived with her grandmother, the matriarch of the House of Magdala, their closest ally among the families that first settled the city. Once his father got over his shock, might he wish the two of them well in their new life together?

"Care to join us, Jacob?" His father's lined face formed a rare smile.

"Yes, of course." Maybe his father would surprise him since he seemed in such good spirits this evening. Then Jacob could return to his beautiful bride within the hour.

A painting of his father and their late mother hung near the small table set for three.

"What do we have here?" Peter lifted the silver lids. "Quail. The kitchen went all out for you, Father."

Jacob sat down in front of a headless bird.

"It's only appropriate the three of us dine in private tonight." Their father reached for his napkin.

"I couldn't agree more." Peter took his seat across from Jacob.

Their father offered a quick prayer, then turned to Jacob. "I have some good news."

"What a happy coincidence." Peter raised his wine goblet. "So does Jacob."

"Yes..." Jacob took a deep breath. "I need to tell you something that—"

"I look forward to hearing all about it, but first I must

confess I had an ulterior motive for going to Lusannah." He passed the basket of bread to Jacob. "While there, I visited an old school friend and met his charming family. He has a teenage son and a daughter just a year younger than you."

Jacob tore off a piece of bread and shoved it in his mouth. Unfortunately, this seemed to be one of those rare occasions when his father was in a talkative mood.

"Her father and I agreed you two would make an excellent match."

"What?" Jacob's mouth went dry, and he couldn't seem to chew.

Peter's eyebrows shot up. "A wife for Jacob...that is good news."

"Yes, they're a highly respectable family, and Lenora comes with a substantial dowry. Her quiet grace reminded me of your mother."

Jacob followed his father's loving gaze to the portrait on the wall and the mother he never knew.

"But are you sure she's not too good for Jacob?" Peter rubbed his chin. "Maybe someone of lower station would be better."

Their father chuckled. "Fortunately, there are still those who revere the priestly line and consider it an honor to marry into the House of Eleazar. The whole family will be visiting in a couple weeks, ostensibly for the younger brother to visit the school. But really, it's an opportunity for you and Lenora to get to know each other."

Jacob forced down his mouthful of bread. "They're coming here?"

"Yes, and I must say, the brother is an impressive student, especially with his mastery of the forgotten language at such a young age."

"Then you two should get along well," Peter said.

Shut up, Jacob mouthed to him as their father paused to dissect his quail.

Feigning innocence, Peter helped himself to more roasted vegetables.

Jacob picked up his knife and fork but had lost his appetite at the mention of Lenora and her dowry.

"I've given some thought as to how we should entertain them," Father continued. "Perhaps a reception in the garden with the First Families. You could take them to the amphitheater since Lenora is fond of drama."

Jacob groaned under his breath. He sure hadn't bargained for the drama unfolding here tonight. Thankfully, he was blessed already with a loving and considerate wife who valued peace and calm. "I have something important—"

"It would be good for you to be seen in public with her." Father cocked his head. "A ball would be ideal since that will serve as a subtle hint to other families that you'll be betrothed soon."

Peter nodded. "A ball sounds perfect. You love to dance in front of large crowds, don't you, Jacob?"

He gripped his knife. "Father, this is a bad idea."

"Not to worry. We'll announce Peter's engagement first. That will give you time to get used to the idea of becoming a husband."

"I don't need time to get used to—"

"Excellent, then the two of you could be married several months after Peter and Cecilia. It'll be a quieter affair, of course."

His wedding had been a quiet affair, perfect in its simplicity. Not only was Sarah now his beloved wife, but she was also a consecrated member of the House of Eleazar. Unfortunately, breaking the news to his father had just become far more complicated.

"We can't risk showing up Peter's Bethulian in-laws with an elaborate wedding," his father added.

"No, that wouldn't do at all." Peter shook his head. "They're very sensitive about their social hierarchies."

Jacob shoved his knife aside before he flung it across the table at his brother. "I can't marry her, Father."

"You haven't even met her." He reached for his wine goblet. "But I promise you, she's lovely."

"I don't doubt that, but remember me telling you I'd find a wife on my own?"

"I remember." He chuckled. "I just never believed it seeing as how you get so tongue-tied whenever you have to speak to a young lady."

Jacob gritted his teeth. "I can't marry her because I already have a wife."

The room fell silent as their father's confused gaze shifted from Jacob to Peter and back again.

"You already..." He slammed his wine goblet down, red droplets spattering the white tablecloth. "What have you done?"

"I—I married Sarah...who brings the Bread of Life." Jacob pointed across the table. "With help from my dear brother here."

Peter's perfectly proportioned face paled. "Yeah, I joined the two lovebirds in holy matrimony after Jacob twisted my arm. But they're actually quite—"

"Has this marriage been consummated?" their father growled.

"Of course." Jacob threw his napkin on the table.

Peter sniggered. "That's kind of the point, isn't it?"

Father rounded on him. "How could you be so stupid? I leave for a week, and you let him talk you into this?"

Peter winced. "It's not like Jacob's going to become high priest. He's just a teacher, so he doesn't need a showy wife."

Their father turned to Jacob. "It wasn't that long ago you were afraid of your own shadow. I thought we'd have to drag you down the aisle when the time came. But I never imagined you would betray me like this."

"I'm sorry you have such a low opinion of me, Father, but I did not betray you." Jacob rose from the table. "I'm a grown man who married the woman I love. And she loves me back, I might add."

"What do you know of love?" Father nearly toppled his chair as he stood. "And you married a servant. This is unprecedented in the history of our house."

"You can stop pretending. You know who Sarah really is. You know she's Hannah Magdala's granddaughter."

His father's dark eyes flashed. "I know who she was. Now she's just a Taberan servant, and that's all she can ever be."

"So what if everyone thinks she's a servant? I certainly don't want to spend the rest of my life with a shallow snob like Cecilia."

"All right, that was uncalled for." Peter moved to stand between them. "But I really think this can be worked out. Father, when the family comes in a couple weeks, you and I can charm them while Jacob behaves like a boor. He can dump wine on them like he did last month at Thelonius's house." He glanced at Jacob. "That was a nice touch, by the way. Then Lenora and her family will depart, never wanting another thing to do with him."

"You idiot." Father glared at Peter. "Do you ever think anything through?"

Peter recoiled a step. "But really, what are the odds this young lady would be interested in Jacob anyway?"

"You two will be the end of our priestly house." Their father ran his fingers through his graying hair. "I don't know how the House of Eleazar can possibly survive such foolishness and ineptitude." His eyes bored into Jacob's. "And you had to bring

Hannah Magdala into this. Now I'm going to have to smooth things over with her too."

"No, you won't. Hannah was there when we got married. She stood beside Sarah, and she welcomed me into her family."

He staggered backward, clutching the vestment around his neck. "Hannah approved of this?"

"Yes."

He shook his head in disbelief. "How am I going to explain what you've done? You have brought shame on the House of Eleazar."

"I've brought shame on our house?" Jacob took a step toward his father. "You only care about money and appearances. You've let the council push you around for years, and everyone knows it. If anyone's brought shame on our house, it's you."

Peter pressed his palm into Jacob's heaving chest. "You need to settle down."

He flung his brother's arm aside.

Their father's nostrils flared. "Get out."

Peter pushed him toward the stairs. "That's enough. You should go."

Jacob stomped toward the staircase, then paused. "I was wrong about one thing." He turned back to his father. "You don't know Sarah at all."

"I know if the Arcanus clan finds out who she really is, you'll end up a widower too."

3

UNFORGIVEN

After sharing a bed with Jacob for a week, Sarah had slept alone last night. Well, not entirely alone. Alma, the calico cat, spent much of the night curled up at her feet, and the book she fell asleep reading lay next to her pillow. The Book of Deborah was probably not the best choice to encourage a good night's sleep. But it seemed to take her mind off of her throbbing headache, which was a strong indication that things hadn't gone as planned for Jacob's conversation with his father.

She returned the strange little book of prophecies to her nightstand with a vague recollection of being assailed by fire and ash in her dreams. The old book and the calico cat made poor substitutes for her handsome husband, but hopefully he would return to the bakery later this morning to fill her in.

After tidying up her room, she went to the kitchen where Marta was already mixing dough and George was starting the fire in the bread oven. Sarah breathed in the familiar scents of flour and woodsmoke that began her day.

"Good morning, dear." Her grandmother Hannah, her gray

hair in a neat bun, motioned for Sarah to join her at the breakfast table where she was enjoying a cup of tea.

Sarah reached for the tea kettle. "I have a bad feeling things didn't go well for Jacob and the high priest last night."

Her grandmother peered over her teacup. "I think that was a given."

Marta chuckled. "Oh, to have been a fly on the wall for that conversation."

"Maybe I should have gone with him." Sarah rubbed her temple.

"Trust me, it's best that you didn't." Grandmother said. "Jacob has to work things out with his father on his own. And if I know Matthias, it may take him a while to come to terms with Jacob asserting his independence. The man can be rather stubborn." She rose from the table. "But speaking of stubborn old men, I've got a council meeting to prepare for this morning."

Five minutes later, Sarah put on her apron and joined Marta at the long wooden counter. "I just wish I knew what happened last night with his father."

"You and me both." Marta kneaded a ball of yeasty dough.

Sarah pulled out a large mixing bowl from under the counter, then added flour, salt, and water. She swirled her fingers through the watery mixture. When she had the proper consistency, she added the starter dough from the wooden bowl with a flame carved into its side.

By early afternoon, all the risen dough had been divided and shaped into loaves. Marta's husband George, his bald head glistening, tended the bread oven, sliding the dough in with his wide wooden paddle. Sarah was grateful for the familiar routine to occupy her hands, but her mind was focused elsewhere.

How many times had she looked to the cellar door, hoping Jacob would come bounding up the stairs in between classes to sweep her up in his arms? Over the past week, he'd made frequent use of the tunnel between the bakery and the natural cavern beneath the cathedral. The secret passage had served the priesthood well in times of strife...along with her brother Jonah when he almost got himself arrested by the city guard last fall.

As soon as seven perfect loaves had cooled, Sarah loaded her basket with the Bread of Life and set out for the cathedral on the other side of the high stone wall, where she suspected family tension was still running high.

THE LONG LINE at the Tower Gate tried what little of Sarah's patience remained. At last, she shoved her papers into the hands of a soldier. He glanced at them, then waved her through the gate and into the Heights, the exclusive district in the heart of the holy city.

After winding her way through the sprawling market in the Square of the Patriarchs, Sarah entered the cathedral through the side door in the arcade. Her footsteps echoed as she hurried past the gleaming bronze doors to the nave inscribed with *In Spiritu et Veritate*. She slid to a stop in the doorway to Jacob's study. But the room was empty and dark with the drapes drawn. The truth would have to wait, it seemed.

But he wasn't teaching a class at this time of day. She began unloading the fresh loaves of bread in the small alcove outside his study. If he didn't return soon, she'd ring the bell for Jacob's younger cousin, Caleb. Maybe he'd know where her husband was this afternoon.

At the familiar swish of a robe, she whirled around to find Peter, her brother-in-law, striding toward her. At least he wasn't scowling like usual. His grudging acceptance of her was helped by learning that she was Councilwoman Hannah Magdala's granddaughter. Therefore, the blood of one of the great houses flowed in her servant's veins.

"Where's Jacob?" she asked him.

"Um…he's probably almost to the village of Adriel by now."

"What?" Sarah nearly dropped a loaf of bread on her foot. "He's gone?"

"Father sent him to fill in for the ailing priest there."

She dropped her voice. "As punishment for marrying me?"

"Father didn't take the news well." Peter rubbed the back of his neck. "He's furious with Jacob…and me."

"Oh, no." Not that it came as a huge surprise.

He gave a stilted laugh. "We'd better hope that old priest doesn't die, or father may leave Jacob there."

Sarah's chest constricted. It never occurred to her they might live somewhere other than the holy city. "But we don't want to live in Adriel, wherever that is."

"Why would you? It's half-way up the south side of Mount Peniel. In other words, it's in the middle of nowhere and has more goats than people. A strong wind would probably blow the whole village off the mountain."

Sarah covered the bread she'd placed on the silver tray with a linen cloth. Peter would consecrate it later, before the priests' evening prayers.

"But I wouldn't be too worried about that." He attempted a smile. "Jacob can work his healing ministrations, and the old guy will be well in a few days. Then he can come home."

She gripped the handle of her empty breadbasket. "I hope so."

"Besides, he'll have to be back before Lenora and her family arrive in a couple weeks."

Sarah's brow furrowed. "Who?"

Peter cleared his throat. "So, the situation's more complicated than we thought. Father returned from his week of rest convinced he'd found the perfect bride for Jacob."

Her mouth fell open. "What?"

"It seems father all but promised him to the daughter of a former classmate of his."

Sarah's stomach lurched. "And they're coming here?"

"Unfortunately, yes." He glanced down the hallway at the sound of several students near the library. "But we'll do a thorough job of convincing them Jacob's not the man for Lenora." He chuckled. "As boring as he is, that won't be too hard."

Sarah failed to see the humor. "Isn't it enough that he's married to someone else?"

Peter shrugged. "You would think, but father needs to figure out a way to save face with the other family."

"How long will that take?"

"Like I told Jacob, it's probably best he stays away for a while. I've never seen father so angry. It'll give him time to cool down."

"Since when does Jacob heed your advice?"

He lowered his voice. "This is a delicate matter. When word gets out that Jacob married a servant—you—behind father's back, it'll look like the high priest's own son doesn't respect his authority."

"Why should he?" Sarah couldn't help but wonder if the high priest would have been more accepting if she wasn't a servant. If her parents hadn't been murdered and cursed, and she could live openly as an heir to the House of Magdala. Or would she still not be good enough?

Peter tugged at the collar of his robe. "Jacob swore an oath on the Sacred Fire to uphold the Priestly Codex, which requires all priests to honor the authority of the high priest and obey his orders. Failing to do so risks expulsion from the priesthood, which Father threatened this morning."

"No..." Had their marriage jeopardized his place in the priesthood, his true calling in life? "But then what would Jacob do?"

"I don't know." Peter shrugged. "It's not like he's has any other talents."

Sarah stared at the floor. If the high priest was this angry at his own son, he must really despise her.

"But I won't let that happen. I'll make sure Jacob stays here in the holy city since he promised to spend the rest of his days as my assistant and scribe if I married the two of you."

"Oh, that explains your change of heart about me."

"And maybe you're growing on me a little." Peter reached into the pocket of his robe and removed a small envelope. "He asked me to give you this."

She tore it open and scanned her husband's hasty scrawl.

DEAR SARAH,

I wish I could tell you everything went smoothly with my father. The truth is we both lost our tempers, and I said terrible things, which only made the situation worse. Please pray that he can forgive me and peace to will return to the House of Eleazar. I love you more than words can express, and I'll come home to you as soon as possible.

Jacob

TEARS STUNG her eyes as she folded the letter and tucked it in her cloak.

Peter cleared his throat. "If it's any consolation, Jacob is utterly miserable."

Sarah pushed past him to leave. "It's not."

4

EVERY HAND TELLS A STORY

arah shifted on the hard pew as the man responsible for her husband's banishment strode across the nave. Her brother-in-law, who had avoided her ever since handing her Jacob's letter, followed on his father's heels. Although she was now part of the House of Eleazar, apparently neither man felt a duty to see how she was faring in her husband's absence.

At the conclusion of the choir's chant, Peter rose and hung his fragrant censer on the crossbar of the silver scepter. He kneeled to pray in the same spot the three of them had stood a week and a half ago when he joined her and Jacob together in marriage. As husband and wife, they had passed their hands through the Sacred Fire to usher Sarah into the priestly family. Peter had even welcomed her with a brotherly kiss on her cheek.

Yet today neither of them could spare a glance in her direction. Based on her clenched jaw, Grandmother sensed their coldness too, even though she had no such gifting. She relied on decades of wisdom and observation.

Matthias ascended to his wooden pulpit with the black

book Jacob normally carried. He smoothed the silver tassels of his vestment, then opened the holy text.

"Faithful is the living God who calls you, for in due time he will bring it to pass."

Bring what to pass? Sarah had a calling as a peacemaker but had only the vaguest notion of what it meant for her future. And Jacob was a prophesied healer. She glanced to her left at the tall stained-glass of Mount Peniel. Her husband was somewhere on the vast southern slope. She hardly heard a word his father was saying as she longed for him to come home.

Returning her gaze to the Sacred Fire on the scepter, Sarah's hand warmed in remembrance of the strands of light that bound her and Jacob together across time and distance.

When everyone rose around her, it dawned on her that the service was ending. Peter stood on her side of the nave, holding a heaping tray of bread. She followed Marta and George out of their row and toward the front.

Peter's cheeks colored slightly as she stepped up to him, determined to hold out her hand for her blessing. Her eyes widened at the faint glowing strands woven between her fingers and around her hand. She looked up at him and smiled.

Flustered, he dropped a piece of consecrated bread into her palm. "The Bread of Life—may it strengthen and sustain you."

She placed the small morsel in her mouth. Apparently, that was all her priestly family was willing to offer her at present. It would have to be enough.

Sarah returned home after her daily bread delivery to the cathedral. She stowed her empty basket under the long kitchen counter, thankful she'd avoided any encounters with her new father-in-law. Not that he wanted to see her. He made that clear at the Sabbath service a few days ago. Although, she had hoped to find Peter in case he knew when his brother would return. Jacob had been gone for over a week now, longer than the time they'd spent together married.

She picked up a broom from the corner and began to sweep up flour and crumbs. All she could do was continue to pray for peace. If the High Priest of Aclesia was determined to stay angry, what impact could she have, even if she was supposed to be some sort of peacemaker? Sarah bent over her broom handle, weighed down by the nagging thought that maybe they should have waited to talk to Matthias first, or at least delivered the news of their marriage to him in a better way.

Marta burst through the backdoor with sprigs of fresh dill, interrupting her gloomy ruminations. "Come with me to the market. I could use some company."

Sarah groaned. She didn't much care for shopping when she was in a good mood.

"I'll not have you sulking about the house the rest of the day." Marta took the broom from her hand. "We'll be quick."

"Oh, all right."

A few minutes later, they set out for the market with Marta chattering about what a beautiful spring they were having. They turned down a peaceful, tree-lined street on the east side of the city. A young couple entered one of the narrow row houses, the wife carrying a baby in her arms.

Sarah looked around the leafy neighborhood. Maybe she and Jacob could make their home in a quiet area like this. There were probably small gardens behind the houses. She could grow vegetables...and flowers. Hadn't Marta just mentioned something about flowers?

Sarah picked up her pace. They could leave together in the morning, her for the bakery and Jacob to the Tower Gate and Cathedral. Then they could return home together in the evening after occasionally dining with her grandmother, Marta, and George. Maybe the sunshine was having a positive effect because she was feeling more hopeful about the future than she had in days.

"Good gracious, Sarah." Marta paused on the corner.

"What?" She turned to her.

"Have you not heard a word I've been saying?"

"Um...you were talking about spring and something about flowers?"

Marta shook her head. "In all my years, I don't think I've ever seen anyone more lovesick." She lowered her voice. "See the market across the street? Wait for me at the fruit stand, and I'll meet you when I'm done."

"Done with what?"

"With delivering Hannah's message to the flower vendor... for Demetrius."

"Oh..." Sarah scanned the market, wondering what secret business her grandmother had this time with Demetrius, a captain in the city guard and best friend of her late father, Thaddeus. Grandmother, Demetrius, and a handful of others had formed a partnership of sorts in the tragic aftermath of her parents' murder that left Sarah and her brother orphaned and cursed.

Reliqui Fideles, they called themselves, the faithful remnant bound together by trust in each other and the living God. With help from Matthias, they'd smuggled Sarah and Jonah out of the holy city and into hiding in the northern city of Taberah, then later the mountain orphanage. In recent years, the city had taken a dark turn, and now they helped to free victims of the flourishing slave trade.

"Come to think of it, Hannah probably wouldn't be pleased I brought you along." Marta fidgeted with the pocket in her cloak. "Best to not mention it to her."

"Don't worry. I won't."

After a powerful demon targeted Sarah last winter, her

grandmother had become overly protective. Surely, there was no need to add to her many concerns.

"And if anything suspicious happens, you don't know me. Just get back home as soon as possible."

"Wait, what?"

Marta ambled off through the crowd, stopping first to sniff a few scented soaps before moving on to the flower vendor's booth.

Sarah hurried to the fruit stand a couple rows over, but it was too crowded to get a clear view of Marta. She moved down the row, then pretended to look at a display of beaded necklaces and crystal pendants sparkling in sunshine.

Marta selected a bouquet of wild flowers, then approached the proprietor, a young woman with a heart-shaped face framed by straight black hair. Her warm smile seemed at home among her beautiful flowers.

And yet, a shiver snaked up Sarah's spine. She quieted her mind, and the low vibration behind her eyes suggested a nearby darkness...someone harboring hatred, or animosity escalating to rage.

She glanced at the neighboring booths, but nothing appeared amiss. Marta passed her payment to the flower vendor, along with a small envelope, no doubt sealed with green wax and the initials R.F. inside a symbol of a flame.

"You're troubled," said a soothing voice from behind.

Sarah spun around. "What?"

A tall woman with frizzy red hair and a jade green robe studied Sarah. "You have a strange aura...calm." Her thin lip twitched. "Peaceful even. Yet I sense something's bothering you." She leaned closer, her hand running down her gold chain to a pendant of a green cat's eye. "I could recommend just the thing to bring you good luck...in matters of love, perhaps?"

"Thank you, but I don't have any money with me." Besides,

she didn't need luck or money. She just needed High Priest Matthias to accept her.

"Hmm, such a pity." The woman glided away to a customer admiring a rose-colored crystal.

Sarah spotted Marta by the fruit stand, turning in circles looking for her.

"I'm over here." She stood on her tiptoes and waved to Marta.

Stealthy as a cat, the frizzy haired woman reappeared at Sarah's side. "You have unusual lines too, very pure."

"Lines?"

"On your hand. I read palms too." The woman pointed under an awning where two stools sat on either side of a small table. "Why don't you let me read yours?"

"Oh, no thanks." Sarah turned to look for Marta. "I really should be going."

"Perhaps your young man will return to you." The palm reader slid in front of her. "Wouldn't you like to know?"

"I already know he will." Sarah backed away.

The woman gave a sad shake of her head. "With men, one can't be too sure. We should consult your love line."

"I don't have any money, remember?"

The palm reader stepped closer. "For a nice young lady such as yourself...no charge." In the next instant, her long fingers encircled Sarah's wrist.

"I said I'd rather not." She hugged her arm to her torso as the woman's anger flared.

"Every hand tells a story." The palm reader's mouth formed a toothy smile that failed to reach her gray eyes. "Won't you let me read yours?"

Sarah's head throbbed, and her pulse quickened beneath the woman's hot grip. Yet the Sacred Fire burning within her sparked pity for this strange woman. She envisioned the white fire rushing through her veins to her hand, extending an offer of light in the desperate darkness that emanated from the palm reader.

The woman recoiled, her hard eyes flashing. With a whispered snarl, she seemed to grow stronger, twisting Sarah's arm and pulling her closer.

"She's not interested in your concocted divinations, nonsensical murmuring, or whatever else you happen to be peddling." Marta's stubby fingers clamped onto the woman's wrist.

"Maybe we should leave it up to the young lady."

Both women squeezed harder, and Sarah's hand began to go numb. The swirling anger made her stomach churn, but it would serve the palm reader right if she vomited all over her shiny crystals.

"You'll unhand her this instant if you know what's good for you," Marta said in a loud voice.

Customers in adjacent booths turned to stare.

"There's no need to get testy." With a huff, the palm reader let go of Sarah.

She rubbed her reddened wrist where long fingernails had dug into her skin.

The woman tossed her frizzy mane over her shoulders and straightened her green robe. "Perhaps you'll pay me a visit some other time, Miss… I didn't get your name."

"That's because it wasn't offered." Marta glanced at Sarah with a subtle shake of her head.

They left the palm reader scowling and muttering under her breath about *people of the flame*.

Still reeling from the bizarre encounter, Sarah stumbled after Marta to an exit on the far side of the market. Once outside, they walked a few blocks in the wrong direction before picking up their pace and doubling back toward the bakery.

Marta slowed to catch her breath. "You need to be more careful." She thrust the bouquet at Sarah, some of the delicate flowers bruised in the altercation. "That woman is clearly the type to prey on the suffering of others. Giving them false hope...or worse."

"She wouldn't leave me alone. She said I have an unusual aura and pure lines."

Marta shrugged. "Might be a bit of truth to that aura business."

"And how did she know I was troubled?" Was the palm reader able to sense certain emotions too?

"Everyone's troubled about something."

"But in matters of love?"

"A reasonable guess, given your age." Marta glanced over her shoulder. "But if that wench does have any powers of divination, I'll wager they're not from above."

5

JUST WHAT YOU NEED

The door to Jacob's study was open. Sarah stowed her breadbasket in the alcove and crept closer. Her heart leapt when she spotted a familiar cloak thrown over a chair and a stack of papers on the desk.

In the next instant, the high priest's voice drifted down the hallway. Dread seized her.

Sarah scurried into the study and peered around the doorframe. At the far end of the hall, beneath the ornate limestone arch marking an entrance to the school, the high priest came into view. A balding, middle-aged man and a plump woman nodded as Matthias gestured to a tapestry on the wall. Peter joined them, a thin boy in his early teens on his heels. The boy swiveled his head as if awed by the hallowed surroundings. He looked up at Peter who edged away from him, arms crossed over his chest.

Sarah let out a soft gasp when Jacob and a petite young woman in a pale blue dress came around the corner. Lenora. Her soft curls bobbed as she leaned over to comment to Jacob. But he stared straight ahead, his hands behind his back.

The high priest shifted his stance and gestured down the

hall. Sarah ducked her head inside Jacob's study. If the tour ventured this way, she'd come face to face with her hostile father-in-law and the young woman he'd much prefer as his daughter-in-law. Heat rose in her cheeks. And how would she explain her presence in the study? She looked around for a place to hide. The heavy floor-length drapes beside the window were the only possible cover.

Her hammering heart made it difficult to hear what was happening through the archway. She thought Matthias mentioned something about the library. Then shuffling foot-steps sounded again.

Cautiously, Sarah peered down the hall just as Jacob glanced toward his study, his face sullen. He stopped mid stride.

"Go on without me." He backed away from Lenora and the others. "I need something in my study."

The gawking boy stared after Jacob until Peter grabbed him by the collar and yanked him toward the library.

Sarah fought the urge to run to her husband as he quickly closed the distance between them.

He swept her into his arms. "I missed you so much."

"Me too." She took his face in her hands and kissed him. "I love you."

"I love you too, and I promise I'm never leaving you again."

They clung to each other in silence until Sarah whispered, "How much longer will they be here?"

"They leave the day after tomorrow." He released her and smoothed his robe. "But after spending most of today with them, her mother is starting to suspect I'd make a lousy husband for her daughter."

She tapped his chest. "Especially since you're already someone else's husband."

"Thankfully that's true." He brushed a loose strand of hair

from her face. "As you can imagine, Peter's proving very helpful, although I don't enjoy being portrayed as a callous fool."

Sarah's eyes flitted to the doorway. "She's pretty."

"I suppose, but as far as I can tell, she doesn't have an original idea in her head."

"She sounds like a better match for Peter."

"You're right." He laughed. "Lenora's brother keeps trying to show off his knowledge of the forgotten language, and Peter doesn't understand half of what he's saying."

Under the circumstances, Sarah couldn't fully appreciate the humor of Peter being shown up by a boy half his age.

"I'd better go, or Father will be suspicious." He planted a soft kiss on her lips. "But I'll come see you tomorrow night right after evening prayers. Save some dessert for me."

Then Sarah was alone again, listening to her husband's footsteps as he hurried to catch up to the attractive visitor and her family.

RAIN DRUMMED a steady beat on the roof as Sarah stared at her half-eaten custard. Jacob's favorite dessert sat congealing at the empty place next to her at the table.

George licked his spoon. "That sure was delicious."

"It was one of your better efforts, dear," Marta added.

Tears pricked Sarah's eyes. "He's not coming."

"Now, we don't know that for sure," Grandmother said.

Sarah glanced at the clock in the corner. "Evening prayers ended half an hour ago. He should be here by now."

A boom of thunder sounded in the distance.

"She's very pretty," Sarah said.

Grandmother pursed her lips. "Yes, you mentioned that."

Sarah looked out the darkened window. But even worse than Lenora being pretty, she seemed normal, with normal looking parents who interacted cordially with the high priest. Maybe Jacob would've been better off with a wife who didn't have to hide her identity, who would fit in with his family and the other First Families. Had her love for him made her selfish? "Maybe he should've married someone like Lenora instead of me."

"Oh, hush. He's madly in love with you." Marta poured Grandmother another cup of tea.

"Yeah, you two were made for each other," George added.

"The high priest hates me, and Peter barely tolerates me."

Grandmother turned to Sarah, her hazel eyes pained. "I don't think it's as bad as all that."

Marta patted her arm. "I know just what you need. A nice warm bath."

Sarah shook her head. "What if the high priest never accepts me as part of his family?"

"Then Matthias is a hard-hearted fool." George scowled.

"And how will I possibly have anything in common with Peter's fancy wife from Bethuliah?" She propped her elbow on the table and rubbed her forehead. "She'll probably loathe me too."

Grandmother reached for her tea. "By the time Peter gets married next summer, I'm sure all of this acrimony will be behind us."

"Yes, you'll probably be one happy family by then." Marta gathered up the empty custard bowls.

Sarah swiped at a tear escaping down her cheek.

"And besides, you and Jacob are adults who can make their own decisions." Grandmother motioned to Marta. "Although maybe a bath is a good idea."

"I'll go draw one." She hurried off to the back hall.

"Matthias can be stubborn as a mule," Grandmother said. "He just needs a little more time to come to his senses."

"But how long will that take?"

Grandmother pursed her lips. "I wish I knew."

Sarah let out a sigh. Was grudging acceptance all she could hope for? Growing up an orphan, she had dreamt of so much more.

LAMPLIGHT SPILLED from the window of the high priest's study onto the wet flagstones as Jacob crept down the terrace steps. No doubt his father was too angry to sleep after an uncomfortable dinner with his old friend and his family. But at least they would depart the holy city in the morning, convinced their daughter Lenora would be better off marrying anyone but him.

Keeping to the shadows, Jacob rounded the base of the north turret. If his father knew where he was headed, there would be no possibility of forgiveness, only expulsion from the priesthood. He darted across the footpath and followed the dense hedge to the high wall that separated him from Sarah. In the corner, a gnarled tree grew close to the wall. The branches were slick from the rain, but he slowly worked his way up to the top of the wall.

The rain began to fall harder, and his drenched cloak weighed on him, but not nearly as much as the hurt in Sarah's eyes when she'd seen him with Lenora yesterday. And he was genuinely sorry for Lenora, who had arrived in the holy city with high expectations for the two of them. She didn't deserve the cold shoulder from him and snide comments from Peter. Although her younger brother's boasts and transparent attempts to ingratiate himself with their father warranted mockery in Peter's eyes. Unfortunately, the boy still seemed to want to attend the school despite the obvious tension between their two families. Jacob did not relish the thought of ever having him as a student.

Mortar gave way under his foot. His shin scraped the rough

wall as a chunk of stone fell with a thud. He stifled a curse, clinging to the wall so he wouldn't topple into a stranger's garden. Nearby a dog began barking.

After regaining his balance, he inched along in a crouch until he spied Marta and George's cottage at the back of Hannah's deep yard.

A couple minutes later, he lowered himself to a seated position, then dropped the rest of the way to the ground, his boots sinking deep into a newly planted bed. Yet another reason for them to be unhappy with him.

Wiping the rainwater out of his eyes, he ran toward the light of the kitchen window and peered in through a gap in the curtains. Hannah sat at the table with Marta and George, but he didn't see Sarah.

Alma the cat huddled under the eave, but she fled into the bushes when he approached like a specter in the night.

He banged on the back door with his fist. After a long moment of silence, George flung open the door, his club drawn and expression fierce. The bedraggled cat scurried into the house.

"Well, well." George lowered his club. "Look what the cat drug in."

Jacob shook himself off as best he could before stepping into the kitchen.

"It's about time you showed up." Marta tossed him a dish towel. "Your poor wife is heartbroken."

"Where is she?" Jacob ran the towel over his face and hair.

"She's in the bath...hopefully calming down."

"For heaven's sake," Hannah said, "what's going on between you and your father?"

He shook his head. "I've never seen him so angry. He says I betrayed him. But I'm going to tell him tomorrow that I refuse to be separated from Sarah any longer. He can exile me to a distant village as punishment, but I won't go without her. And if he expels me from the priesthood, so be it. I can find some other work."

Hannah held up a bony hand. "Surely it doesn't need to come to anything so drastic. I just got my granddaughter back, and I don't want to lose her again." She glanced at the back hallway. "Nor do I enjoy seeing her hurt."

Jacob winced. "Neither do I."

"Please inform your father tomorrow that I wish to speak with him soon...in private."

"I will." He nodded hopefully. "Thank you."

"Well, are you going to stand there dripping muddy water all over my clean floor," Marta said, "or are you going to see your wife?"

Jacob looked down at his soaked clothes, and his mouth curled into a grin. Maybe he could use a bath too.

6

BROTHERS OVER BREAKFAST

Sarah woke to the clatter of mixing bowls in the kitchen. Jacob's long arm was draped around her waist, his chin resting on top of her head. She closed her eyes again, remembering last night when he'd surprised her in the bath, kneeling next to the tub to kiss her, then taking the washcloth...

He thrashed in his sleep. "No..." he mumbled, "not father."

She squeezed his arm. "Jacob, wake up."

"What?" he said with a start. "What time is it?"

Sunlight streamed in from the small window. "I think we overslept."

He reached for his pocket watch on the nightstand and groaned. "Oh, no. I slept right through morning prayers." He fell back on the pillows. "Peter better have made some excuse for me. I've covered for him enough times."

She brushed his stubbly cheek with a kiss and whispered, "Since you don't have to teach a class for a couple hours, you could stay for breakfast."

"Now that's an offer I can't refuse."

Half an hour later they were dressed and in the kitchen.

"Marta, why didn't you wake us earlier?" Sarah sliced several pieces of bread.

She winked. "Oh, I figured you could use the extra time together after being apart for two weeks."

"That was sweet of you." Sarah brought the bread to Jacob at the table.

"What can I say?" Marta flipped her ball of dough over. "I'm just a sucker for young love."

"Me too." He pulled Sarah onto his lap and nuzzled her neck.

The backdoor opened, and her brother Jonah strode in with a bag of flour on his shoulder. He jerked to a stop, his mouth falling open. The bag of flour landed at his feet, sending up a white cloud. "What the—"

"Jonah, it's not what you're thinking." Sarah leapt up. "Well, it is, but I can explain."

"Morning, Jonah," Marta called from the end of the counter.

His eyes darted to Marta, then back to Jacob.

"Oh, perhaps this would be a good time for a family chat." Marta wiped her hands on a towel. "I'll just excuse myself to the parlor."

Jonah stepped over the bag of flour on the floor. "Sarah, what are you doing with—with him?"

"We got married a few weeks ago." She pressed her hand on Jacob's shoulder as a subtle warning to let her manage Jonah before his shock flared into another fistfight like the first time the two of them met. "It was kind of sudden, but we're so happy together."

"You married a priest?" Jonah threw up his hands. "You couldn't marry some normal fellow?"

Sarah hurried to the counter to cut two extra thick slices of bread for her brother. "I didn't fall in love with a normal fellow."

He took the plate from her. "And you didn't even invite me to your wedding."

"I am sorry about that." She was all too familiar with the sting of rejection and exclusion.

"If it makes you feel any better, we didn't invite my father either." Jacob propped his elbow on the table. "But I hope you won't be as mad as he is. He banished me to a village in the middle of nowhere for a couple weeks as punishment."

"Wait, you married Sarah behind your father's back?" Jonah's mouth quirked into a crooked grin. "The high priest, right?"

"Yeah, and he's still barely speaking to me. Although that's not all bad."

Jonah gave an approving nod before shoving half a slice of bread in his mouth.

"How did you get here last night, anyway?" Sarah sat next to Jacob, thankful they'd avoided another confrontation.

"I snuck out the back of the cathedral and climbed a tree in the cemetery to the top of the wall. There was an unfriendly dog a block over that had me worried though."

"Why didn't you just go through that tunnel?" Jonah asked through a mouthful of bread.

My father forbade me to use the tunnel to go see Sarah." He laughed. "But he didn't say I couldn't use it to return, which I should do soon since I still have homework to grade this morning."

"So, let me get this straight." Jonah pointed at him with a crust of bread. "You snuck out of the cathedral last night to bed the bread girl."

Sarah scowled at him. "I'm his wife."

Jacob reached for her hand. "You'll always be the bread girl to me."

Marta peeked into the kitchen. "Jonah, when you're done

visiting with your sister, Hannah would like to speak with you upstairs in her study."

"Me?" Blood drained from his face. "Why?"

Marta shrugged. "Must be something important, but it's not my business to ask."

"Am I in trouble? I haven't even done anything bad lately." He cocked his head, eyes distant. "At least, I don't think so."

Sarah stifled a laugh. As much as Jonah was surprised about her marriage to Jacob, that was nothing compared to what their grandmother was about to reveal to him concerning their family history. "I'd brace yourself if I were you."

Jacob nodded with priestly seriousness. "Probably best just to get it over with, whatever it is."

"But now that you're my brother-in-law, you could put in a good word for me, right? Hannah seems to like you."

"I don't know..." Jacob rubbed his chin. "I seem to recall the last time I tried to help you, you punched me in the mouth."

7

DISRUPTED PLANS

Sapientia et Officium...wisdom and duty. Hannah glanced at the inscription above the double doors to the school. Hopefully she could impart some wisdom to the high priest who regarded his youngest son as failing in his duty to marry the woman he deemed appropriate. But seeing how Matthias had put her off for over a week, she wasn't optimistic.

Jacob waited for her in the entryway.

"How would you assess your father's mood this afternoon?" she asked in a low voice.

"About the same as the last few weeks, I'm afraid." He escorted her past the library where adolescent boys bent over their books at long tables overlooking the leafy courtyard.

"I'll do my best to improve the situation for all our sakes," she said as they turned down the rear hallway toward the high priest's study.

"We really appreciate your help," he whispered, then knocked on the open door. "Madam Magdala's here to see you, Father."

"Come." The high priest rose from his chair.

Jacob turned on his heels and sped down the hall, leaving her standing on the threshold.

Taking a deep breath, she strode across the plush burgundy rug. A tray of tea and honey cakes sat on the corner of the high priest's desk. At least he'd gone to the trouble of requesting tea service from the kitchen.

He gestured to a chair in front of his desk. "To what do I owe the pleasure?"

"Come now, Matthias." Hannah took her seat. "We go back a long way."

"Yes, we do." He reached for the silver tea pot. "So imagine my surprise when I learned my son had married your grand-daughter behind my back, knowing full well I had other plans for him."

"Apparently Jacob and Sarah had plans of their own." Hannah accepted her tea from the frowning priest.

He reclined in his high-backed chair and stared at her over steepled hands. "Jacob is caught up in a young man's desires. And Peter's always been gullible with a bit of a rebellious streak. An unfortunate combination. But you, my old friend... how could you let this happen?"

"I admit I was caught off guard when Sarah told me their intentions the night before the wedding." She shook her head. "And poor Sarah was caught off guard even more when I confessed that I was her grandmother and had sent her and her brother into hiding when they were small children."

Her eyes stung, recalling how they had wept together over the painful story of her parents' death and the heinous curse placed upon Sarah and Jonah by Niccolus Arcanus. But the next day their sorrow gave way to the joy of Sarah's marriage to Jacob.

"As for stopping those two falling in love, I could no more hold up my hand and stop the wind."

"This would have been a valuable alliance with a prominent family in Lusannah," Matthias said.

She reached for her tea cup. "Maybe so, but you're hardly the first father to disapprove of his son's choice for a wife."

"It's one thing to lose the opportunity to another family of high standing, but to a servant…"

Hannah pursed her lips. "I would remind you this is my granddaughter you're speaking of."

"Yes, but you cannot claim her now."

"That doesn't mean I love her any less."

He narrowed his eyes. "It seems to me you've put her in a dangerous position by bringing her back to the holy city. If the House of Arcanus learns she's still alive, what then?"

"They can never know." Her hand trembled slightly as she set her tea cup on the saucer. "Thankfully, Jacob is content to remain in the background. And when the Arcanus clan eventually hears the news that he married a Taberan servant, they'll just turn their noses up at your house all the more."

He scowled. "If that's even possible. I know we covered our tracks well, but others are at risk too. If they discover who she's been with all these years—"

"What's done is done." Hannah took a slow breath. "Now Sarah and Jacob are bound together by a higher authority than you."

He pinched the bridge of his nose. "Yes, unfortunately."

"The question remains, what do we do now?" She selected a honey cake, then slid the plate to Matthias with the hope that a sweet treat might improve his disposition. "Pretending they're not married is not a long-term solution. If you're bound and determined to hold a grudge, I can't stop you, but I seem to recall you preaching about forgiveness last Sabbath."

With a groan, the high priest reached for a cake. "This situation will be distasteful to the Bethulians. They're very particular about social hierarchies and their customs."

"I don't see what bearing that should have on Sarah and Jacob." She poured herself a second cup of tea since he seemed unable to attend to rudimentary hospitality. "Honestly, I know you want to get off on a good foot with Peter's in-laws, but their daughter is marrying into your house."

"Actually, I've given this problem considerable thought in recent days." He drummed his fingers on his desk. "Next month, Peter and I will travel to Bethuliah so he can formally propose to Cecilia and commence their betrothal period. After the excitement dies down in a few months, we can quietly announce Jacob's marriage."

"That sounds sensible." And about the best she could hope for from Matthias.

"I'm still tempted to send him and Sarah off to a village until Peter's wedding as punishment."

"For that, I would never forgive you."

He waved his hand. "An idle threat... Peter represents the future of the priesthood, but he needs Jacob by his side to compensate for his scholarly shortcomings and impulsiveness. Strange though, I always thought he'd be the one to lose his head over a beautiful girl, not Jacob."

She chuckled. "Jacob has surprised us both. In the meantime, will you allow him to use the tunnel to see Sarah? So he doesn't risk breaking his neck scaling the wall."

"Yes, yes." He stroked his beard. "You know, Jacob could have become a renowned healer. His reputation will be tarnished by going behind my back to marry a servant."

"Maybe with the First Families, but those most in need of healing don't reside in the Heights, nor would they care about Sarah's fictitious pedigree." She took a sip of tea. "I have no doubt Jacob will be a great priest in many respects, but my granddaughter has a calling as well. Do you not remember the prophecy you spoke over her as a baby?"

"What prophecy?" He brushed a crumb from his desk.

"About her being blessed with a spirit of peace." Hannah straightened. "Are you telling me you've forgotten?"

"I can't recall every utterance over every infant I've blessed."

"Then let me refresh your memory since I was standing right next to Rebecca. 'This child is blessed with a spirit of peace. What she prays through trials and tears will bring forth an inheritance of peace in her years.' Those were your exact words. I suggest you reflect on them before you dismiss Sarah as just another thorn in your side."

"An inheritance of peace…" He sighed. "I would very much like to preside over such a time. Maybe she can use her gift to bring peace to the council. That would be quite an accomplishment."

"Indeed, but I suggest you make peace with your son as a start. Why put him through the torment of separation from his wife?" Hannah twisted the silver band on her finger and sighed. "The years may dull the pain of loss, but they don't erase it."

The high priest who'd spent almost half his life as a widower folded his hands on his desk. "No, they don't."

"Sarah and Jacob are good for each other, Matthias. Why not let them be happy? We never know what life will bring."

8

A MOTHER'S BLESSING

The summer sun beat down on Jacob as he crouched in front of the weathered tombstone and traced his finger over the ornate letters visible above the weeds. *Marissa Eleazar, Beloved Wife and Mother...* He tore at a vine that snaked up the stone. How long had it been since he'd visited her grave? He yanked the thick weeds out of the dry ground. The date of her death...and his birth...stared him in the face. Gone at only twenty-five years old, the same age as Peter now.

Jacob flung the uprooted weeds onto the stone path.

A black robed priest stood a few yards up the hill.

"I saw you walking through the garden from my window," his father said. "Given what today is, I had a hunch as to where you were going."

Jacob picked up a downed branch and threw it on the pile of debris. Later he would set fire to all that defaced his mother's grave.

His father stepped closer. "I suppose I should wish you a happy birthday."

Jacob shook his head at the obligatory sentiment. "This

hasn't been a happy day for the House of Eleazar in twenty-one years."

The creases in his father's face deepened. "It's a day that holds both gladness and grief, to be sure."

Jacob glanced at the towering oak next to the eastern wall. When he was a young boy, his father made Peter take him to their mother's grave once a month. After an awkward silence, they'd run toward the oak and escape through the secret hole in the wall behind the underbrush. There he and Peter would sit with their backs to the graveyard and look out over the valley, imagining adventures in the land beyond.

His father cleared his throat. "I know you think I've been unduly harsh, selfish even, in my attempts to find good matches for you and Peter."

Jacob turned to him, their uneasy truce of the last couple months in jeopardy.

"But I also wished to protect you." He reached down and brushed dirt from the top of his wife's gravestone. "Marrying for love comes with its own risks, and it can inflict wounds no one should have to bear."

"I'm willing to take those risks for Sarah."

"It seems your wife attracts enemies, of both the mortal and immortal variety."

"I can protect her." He'd saved her from the versarius last winter, although he and Peter nearly lost their lives in the process. He tugged at his collar. Recently Sarah seemed to be experiencing some of the same symptoms as when that darkness drew near.

"By all accounts, you're becoming a great healer." His father sighed. "But not even you can cheat death."

As Jacob stared at the lined face of the man who'd been left alone to raise two young boys, he knew he would do everything in his power to cheat death if Sarah was in peril.

His father crossed his arms over his chest, hands hugging

his sides. "A few months before you were born, I had the most vivid vision of your hands alight with flame. Whoever you touched was restored to health. I knew then you'd become a powerful healer, such as we haven't seen in Aclesia in hundreds of years. Your mother was so excited and proud."

"I know." Jacob kicked at a stone on the dry ground. "You told me that many times growing up. I just never lived up to it, or even believed it, until Sarah believed in me. She made it possible."

His father stroked his graying beard. "The love of a good woman can bring out our best. And I don't doubt that Sarah is a good woman."

"Then why do you reject her?"

"Under different circumstances, she might have made a good match for you since she comes from a respectable house. On her mother's side, at least."

"But now that she can't claim her lineage in the House of Magdala, she's not good enough?"

"There are those on the council who would like to weaken us because they see us as a check on their power and ambitions. When the news of your marriage becomes public, they'll distort the facts and spread unsavory rumors. That she seduced you, perhaps, to elevate her station."

"She did no such thing."

"Of course." His father's expression darkened. "But we can neither risk exposing her true identity, nor underestimate the treachery of the House of Arcanus."

"I know that." Jacob took a slow breath to calm his racing heart. "I can live the rest of my life in Peter's shadow as long as I'm with Sarah. My hope is that you can be content with that too."

He gave a slight nod. "I think your mother would be proud of the man, and the healer, you've become."

Jacob swallowed the lump in his throat. "Thanks." But

would she approve of the husband he'd become? Would she have accepted Sarah? His eyes stung as he stared at her tombstone. How might things have been different had she survived his birth twenty-one years ago?

"I never told you, but your mother spoke of another vision right before she died." A shadow passed over his father's face. "She'd lost a lot of blood, and I thought she was confused, delirious even. Her voice was so weak that I had to bend my head close to hear. I should have known then what she knew... that she was dying." He gazed at Mount Peniel in the distance. "Maybe I did know and just couldn't accept it."

Jacob blinked a few times. On her deathbed, his mother had a vision, and this was the first he was hearing of it? "What was her vision?"

His father's eyes glistened as he turned away from the holy mountain. "She saw you as a grown man wearing a white robe. She said you were leading a huge multitude, with people crowding around you, calling out to you."

Jacob staggered backward, snapping a twig as an image flashed through his mind. "No, that can't be." Strangers reaching for him and calling his name was like something out of a dream...or a recent nightmare. "She must have meant Peter. He's a natural leader and the future high priest, not me."

"Of course, I assumed she was speaking of Peter, but your mother insisted it was you." His father cleared his throat. "I can still picture her kissing your forehead as you slept on her chest. 'Be blessed, my beautiful boy,' she whispered in your ear. Then she looked at me and said softly, 'Goodbye, my love,' and slipped away from us."

Standing at her grave, Jacob realized just how little he knew of the woman who had given him life. The flesh and blood woman who had walked these grounds and called the cathedral home. Did she have other spiritual gifts too, like his own wife? Had he reduced his mother to a caricature in his mind to guard against the acute loss he shared with his father and brother?

But as for her vision of him leading a great multitude, he prayed it would never come to pass because he needed to shield Sarah from scrutiny. And aside from his weekly healing service, the only thing he aspired to lead was his own family.

9

———

HANNAH'S SUSPICION

As summer gave way to fall, Jonah arrived at the bakery with a load of freshly milled flour from the village. Now that he knew Hannah was their grandmother and not just a kind benefactor, Sarah and Grandmother surprised him with a birthday lunch for his seventeenth birthday.

Although he ate every last bite of the beef stew and apple cobbler served him, he was less enthusiastic about his practical presents of clothing from Marta and George, a pocket watch from Grandmother, and a wide brimmed hat from Sarah to conceal his face that had come to bear a strong resemblance to their late father.

Jacob gave him a book of adventure stories, which probably didn't rate much better. "I'm sure you'll have read those by the next time I see you."

"I wouldn't count on it." Jonah looked around the kitchen. "But thanks for all my gifts."

Sarah hugged him goodbye, grateful he had the maturity to offer muted thanks, at least.

As he gathered his things to return to Havilah, Grandmother rose from the table. "There's one last item you might be more fond of, although I have mixed feelings about it."

Jacob glanced at her, but Sarah shrugged in confusion at the unexpected development.

A few moments later, Grandmother returned from the parlor with a long, thin bundle wrapped in coarse black cloth.

"Is this—?" Jonah's eyes widened in wonder as he uncovered the scratched and dented pommel of a broad sword.

The black cloth fluttered to the floor.

"Demetrius kept your father's sword all these years," Grandmother told him. "We thought you should have it now."

Jonah's hand closed around the hilt of their father's humble sword. Mesmerized, he drew the blade from its leather sheath imprinted with the small flame of the holy city's guard corp. In the next instant, he assumed a fighting stance, waving the sword as if defending against an unseen foe.

Everyone within ten feet of him recoiled.

"Put that away, or take it out back before you run someone through," Grandmother said sharply.

"Come on." George shooed him toward the door. "A sword's not my favorite weapon, but I can teach you a few basics."

"I'm not so sure about this." Sarah watched through the window as George improvised with a garden hoe.

Jacob laughed. "Yeah, that hoe's a goner."

Jonah parried another blow, reveling in the sword play.

"You didn't eat much." Marta picked up Sarah's plate. "Are you feeling poorly again?"

"My stomach's just a little upset."

Marta handed Jacob her apple cobbler with one bite taken out of it. "It would be a shame for this to go to waste."

"You don't look sick." Jacob stabbed at the cobbler. "But you have been really tired lately."

"Please don't tell me there's another dark spirit about," Marta said from the sink. "I think we've all had enough of that."

Ever since her disturbing encounter with the palm reader, something pricked at Sarah's consciousness. But she couldn't put a name to it, that darkness just beneath the surface. Unlike the versarius, it was diffuse, as if it came from many directions. Or was it just her imagination?

"Have you been having headaches again?" Jacob asked.

Sarah shook her head. "No, not lately." But her stomach had been unsettled for the past week, and her chest was sore. That much wasn't her imagination.

"Your face looks a little flushed." He ran his palm across her forehead. "But you don't feel feverish."

"Yesterday morning you got queasy while we were mixing dough." Marta returned with more tea. "That's not like you."

Sarah took a tentative sip of tea.

Grandmother studied her from the head of the table. "Might there be a more natural explanation?"

"What do you mean?" she asked.

"Well, you have been married for over four months now." Grandmother lowered her voice. "When was the last time you bled?"

Sarah's cheeks warmed. "Umm...when we had dinner with Thaniel and Cornelia."

"That was five weeks ago."

"What?" Her face blazed. "Are you sure it was that long?"

"Positive." Grandmother nodded.

"Oh..." Sarah looked down at her belly. But wasn't there a lingering curse of infertility on the city courtesy of the sorcerer Cedrian? She turned to her husband in disbelief.

His brown eyes glistening, Jacob wrapped his arm around her shoulder. "You could be..."

Despite her shock, the hopeful joy on his face made Sarah love him all the more. Of course, he wouldn't be the one to give birth.

Marta clapped her hands together. "It would be so delightful to have a baby around again."

"Do you know what this means?" He pulled Sarah closer. "My father will have to let us make our marriage public, and then we can find a home for ourselves and our baby." He glanced at Grandmother. "Not that we don't appreciate everything you've done for us, of course."

"I know." She nodded, cradling her cup of tea. "But let's not get ahead of ourselves."

"You could bring the baby here just like your mother used to bring you when she helped me bake bread," Marta exclaimed.

Warmth flooded Sarah's chest, remembering the love of her mother in that fleeting vision from her Anointing in the spring. Could she have that depth of love for her own child? Assuming she was carrying a child. She had the sudden urge to run to the old bassinet and rocking chair in the basement.

"Gracious, I imagine the child of a peacemaker and healer will be quite extraordinary," Marta said.

Grandmother's tea cup clanked on its saucer. "Indeed..." she murmured.

Sarah was vaguely aware of heavy footsteps and the kitchen door slamming.

"What's going on?" Jonah asked.

"Did we miss something?" George's sweaty face crinkled with concern.

Sarah took a deep breath. "I—I might be expecting a baby."

"Well, well." George broke into a wide grin and clapped Jacob on the back.

"Huh," said Jonah still clutching his sword. "I bet I'd make an excellent uncle."

Jacob shook his head. "Only if we want another trouble-maker in the family."

10

HOUSE OF BREAD

At the sound of a knock on the front door, Sarah looked up from shaping her ball of dough.

"Who would be calling at eleven o'clock in the morning?" Marta glanced out the back window at George chopping more wood for the bread oven.

Sarah wiped her hands on her apron and headed for the hallway. "I'll find out."

"Maybe you should let George—"

"Hi, Thaniel." Sarah opened the door for her grandmother's old friend and founding member of Reliqui Fideles. A bulging satchel was slung over his shoulder. "What are you doing here?"

He stepped into the front hall and pointed up the stairs to her grandmother's study. "I was summoned."

"Oh. Can I take your cloak?"

He dropped his satchel at his feet and handed Sarah his gray cloak. "What a heavenly smell."

"Would you like some tea and bread? We'll have fresh loaves coming out of the oven soon."

He patted his ample belly. "I never refuse an offer of the Bread of Life."

"Good morning, Thaniel," Marta said as they entered the kitchen. "What brings you by today?"

"Actually, I don't know." He warmed his hands by the bread oven. "Hannah was rather cryptic in her note."

Grandmother's clipped steps in the hallway suggested she was coming to retrieve the portly scholar of the Forgotten Language.

"But I suspect I'll find out shortly."

"Good, you're here," Grandmother said by way of greeting.

"Yes, my nose led me straight to the kitchen."

"Sarah can bring us tea later." Grandmother's expression indicated that whatever business she had with Thaniel, she wanted to get right to it.

SEATED BEHIND HER WALNUT DESK, Hannah moved her quill and inkwell off to the side by a thick stack of ledgers that would require much attention later. But for now, she could think of nothing other than her outlandish theory that a part of her hoped wasn't true. She trusted Thaniel to give her his honest opinion, even if it meant telling her she was crazy.

"You wanted to know about prophecies on the Convergence." Thaniel dug through his satchel. "I'm intrigued, to say the least."

Hannah twisted the silver band on her finger. "Specifically which writings pertain to the coming of the Heir."

"Well, the Fourth Scroll, of course." His jowls quivered as he chuckled. "And wouldn't we all love to know what that says."

"Yes...but what about the mother of the Heir to the Sacred Fire? I don't recall ever hearing anything on that topic."

He shook his head. "No, you wouldn't have since there's

very little to go on." He placed a dusty book on her desk. "Although there's one controversial prophecy from Ezra."

Hannah took a deep breath. "And that would be what?"

He flipped through the yellowed pages. "It should be in this collection... Ah, yes. Ode to the Exalted Mother. Shall I read it?"

She leaned forward. "Please."

EXALTED IS she who extends her hand to the downtrodden,
   and supplies bread to both rich and poor.
   She wears wisdom like a crown of gold,
   And on her lips are words of life and peace.
   Her house will be a place of love and laughter,
   And the son of her womb will be seated above all the elders
of the land.
   He will judge with fairness and rule forever in right-
eousness,
   And her name shall be eternally blessed.

"WORDS OF LIFE AND PEACE," Hannah whispered.

"Beautiful, isn't it?" Thaniel leaned back, tugging on his tight vest.

"Indeed." She blinked back the moisture gathering in the corners of her eyes. "But what makes it controversial?"

"For centuries, it was thought to be about the mother of the Heir, since the text indicates he will *rule forever*. But that view seems to have fallen out of favor. Now scholars think it's just an example of a virtuous woman of faith. Although, personally, I'm inclined to believe the former."

"You are... That's good." She rubbed the back of her neck. "As am I. Thaniel..."

He looked up from his beloved book.

"My granddaughter, the peacemaker, is pregnant."

"Oh, how wonder—"

Blood drained from his broad face. "What?"

"She's almost two months pregnant and downstairs baking bread at this very moment."

His eyes darted to the prophetic passage from Ezra again.

Laughter sounded below, and then light footsteps on the staircase.

He drew in a sharp breath. "She's coming up."

"Yes, along with the baby in her womb."

He lowered his voice. "Does she know?"

"No," she whispered. "The poor girl just got used to the idea of being pregnant."

Thaniel shut the book, his fingers drumming on the cover as Sarah entered the room with a tray of tea. She set the tray on the desk in front of Hannah then passed him a plate with two slices of bread and a small jar of honey.

"This is fresh out of the oven, and we have another loaf downstairs for you to take home to Cornelia."

"How very thoughtful of you." His hand trembled so much, the honey nearly slid off the plate.

She extended her hand and caught the jar before it tumbled onto the desk.

"Dear me." A sheen of sweat appeared on Thaniel's lined forehead. "Pardon this clumsy old scholar."

She laughed. "You'll be in big trouble if you get honey on Grandmother's desk."

"You're quite right, dear." Hannah reached for her tea cup.

"Heaven knows, I don't need any more trouble." He removed a handkerchief from his breast pocket and dabbed at his brow.

"No need to come back up for the dishes. I'll bring them down when I show Thaniel out."

"I'll get back to work then." Sarah waved at them from the doorway, a smudge of flour on her wrist.

"Can it really be?" He glanced toward the stairs. "Our Sarah?

"Based on her gifting as a peacemaker, the versarius hunting her last winter, and what you've just told me, how can it not be?"

He blew out a breath. "And then there's Jacob's growing power as a healer."

"Yes, that too." She set her cup down with a clink. "But one thing doesn't seem to make sense. Wouldn't you expect the Heir to be fathered by Peter, instead of Jacob?"

"Not necessarily. If Peter doesn't have a son, then succession moves down the birth order to Jacob and his eldest son. It would hardly be the first time that's happened in the House of Eleazar." He tugged at his whiskers. "Besides, would Patrimus really want Peter raising the long-awaited Heir?"

"A fair point." Hannah cocked her head. "But I wonder what that portends for Peter and how he'll take the news?"

"He does have quite the ego." Thaniel reached for a piece of bread. "But based on a strict reading of the Scroll of Prophecy, the Heir could be any male with the blood of Eleazar, no matter how distantly related to the current high priest. That's certainly the hope of many of the priestly orders, like the Taberans who believe the Heir will come from Joshua's descendants."

She glanced out the window to the north. "I fear their disappointment may revive tensions in what's been a fraught relationship historically."

He nodded. "The high priests have always held that the Heir to the Sacred Fire will be a direct descendant of the high priest alive at the time, and therefore heir per both the original covenant and the Priestly Codex. The traditionalists believe those two foundational documents can't contradict each other. But the Codex was written by Eleazar late in his life, so it doesn't carry the same weight as the Sacred Scrolls, especially with those outside the holy city."

He reached for his satchel. "Shall I read the text from the Second Scroll?"

She waved her hand. "That won't be necessary."

"I'd guess at least ten percent of the men in the holy city can trace their lineage back to one of the high priests. And many others across Aclesia."

Hannah's brow creased. "That may be a good thing."

"How so?"

"If the Heir can come from anywhere, it'll be easier to keep this quiet. I shudder to think how the dark spirits will react."

He paled again. "The versarius was frightening enough."

She leaned back in her chair. "But what if keeping Sarah's pregnancy hidden is part of Patrimus's plan? Maybe we hid her all those years from more than just the Arcanus clan."

Thaniel stroked his gray goatee. "A divine protection of sorts..."

She nodded. "And that begs the question, what now?"

"Does Matthias know of your theory?"

"No, given his injured pride, he won't even acknowledge Sarah as Jacob's wife. And just when it seemed he and Jacob were mending their relationship, he learned of her pregnancy."

"I take it that didn't go over well."

"Apparently he railed about the added complications and the growing likelihood of offending the Bethulians. In their rigid culture, the eldest marries first and has children first."

"Let's hope his worries are overblown," Thaniel said. "They've been loyal allies over the last couple centuries."

"But can they be trusted with knowledge of the coming Heir?" Hannah's shoulders stiffened. "Knowledge that puts Sarah's life in danger?"

"That I don't know." He leaned his chin on a pudgy fist.

"And then there's the matter of the Fourth Scroll... Would Matthias even consent to opening it?"

"He'd have to be convinced there's good reason to, and for that I might need your help."

"Yes, of course." He folded his hands on the desk, his expression pensive. "That's a heavy burden for a young couple to bear."

"Indeed, so don't breathe a word of this to anyone."

11

SONS OF ELEAZAR

arah huddled on the end of the sofa in the parlor, closest to the fireplace. She tightened her shawl around her shoulders. The days were growing shorter, and the coolness in the air threatened winter, even if it was still a couple months off.

Grandmother sat across from her reading a book. Or rather not reading, since she'd open the book, scan a few lines, then put it down again.

"I would have thought the evening prayer service would be over by now." Grandmother removed her spectacles and rubbed her forehead.

"I can't imagine what's taking Jacob so long." Sarah leaned back on the sofa and closed her eyes. "I told him you wanted to talk to us tonight."

"You're not going to fall asleep on me, are you?"

She blinked her eyes open. "No, I'm just so tired. He woke me up in the middle of the night again, mumbling about his father in his sleep."

"Just wait until he's older and begins to snore."

"There's something to look forward to." Sarah groaned. "I

think he's still bothered about his father and their strained relationship, but when I ask him, he doesn't want to talk about it."

"Another common trait of men. But once you get settled somewhere as husband and wife, I expect the bad dreams and worries will lessen."

Sarah pushed herself up. "About that, I'm sure you're wondering how much longer we'll be here."

"That's not why I asked to speak with you both this evening." Grandmother set the book that she'd read little of on the end table. "I don't want you to leave. I treasure having you here, and I so look forward to meeting my first great grandchild. Although it would look awfully strange for my employee to live in my home with her husband, the son of the high priest."

"Yes, that could lead to some unwanted questions." Sarah sighed. The need to keep her identity secret seemed to complicate everything. "But Jacob saw a notice about a place for rent only about twenty minutes from here, near the foundry. I'm going to look at it tomorrow afternoon."

Grandmother frowned. "Maybe I should go with you. That area can be a little rough."

"I'm sure I'll be fine."

"Sarah!" Jacob called from the kitchen.

She turned toward the doorway. "We're in the parlor."

His face flushed, he burst into the room. "I think I had a vision in the Sacred Fire."

"You did?" Sarah made room on the sofa for him. But was the vision cause for celebration, caution, or just confusion? The elation on his face seemed to suggest the first possibility.

"Good heavens. What did you see?" Grandmother asked.

"It was just for a split second, but I saw a young man with his hand on the silver scepter. His face was glowing, and he had dark wavy hair like mine. He turned and looked right at me. I think he's the Heir to the Sacred Fire." He paused to take a breath. "Of course Peter doesn't believe me, probably because he's never had a vision in the fire."

Sarah swallowed. "But what does the vision mean?

"I think it means he's coming soon."

"Yes." Grandmother leaned forward. "I suspect in about six months."

"What?" Sarah looked from her grandmother to her husband.

"Wait…" Jacob's jaw dropped. "Our baby?"

"That can't be," Sarah murmured as she stared at Grandmother. The mother of the Heir could only be someone important, beautiful, and poised. Like Peter's fiancée. Certainly not a quiet servant who was a little odd.

"Please don't look at me as though I'm senile." Grandmother broke the silence.

Jacob gently placed his hand on Sarah's belly. "Maybe it could be our baby."

Sarah didn't know whether to laugh or cry at the notion that Matthias, who couldn't bring himself to acknowledge her as his daughter-in-law, would believe she'd give birth to the long-awaited Heir to the Sacred Fire. She couldn't believe it herself. Besides, the high priest didn't put much stock in his own prophesy that she was blessed with a spirit of peace and her prayers would bring about an inheritance of peace.

She sucked in a breath. "But if that's true, it would mean the end of the age is coming too."

"Yes…" A hint of sorrow shadowed Grandmother's hazel eyes. "But remember, the age to come is Aetas Pacis."

"The Age of Peace," Sarah whispered. But what trials must they endure before then?

Grandmother turned to Jacob. "Do you know the prophecy about the mother of the Heir?"

Sarah's thoughts swirled as she sat in the crook of her husband's arm. He and Grandmother talked excitedly about an old prophet named Ezra. But their rapid-fire words blurred in the background, and she only caught confusing snatches —*bread, peace, son,* and *forever reign.*

Instead of trying to make sense of their conversation, she stared at the low fire in the hearth, its embers glowing orange. Unbidden, different words came to the forefront of her tired and confused mind...the last words ever written by the Prophetess Deborah...*as the present age began in fire, so it will end in fire. But still the vision awaits its time.*

But just how much longer did the vision of a battle between two fires have to wait?

12

A TELLING ENCOUNTER

Sarah and her grandmother set out late the following afternoon in a cool mist. The excitement of finding a new home for her and Jacob was dampened, not just by the poor weather but the shocking prospects that she carried the Heir to the Sacred Fire, the end of the age was fast approaching, and she had a mysterious role to play as a peacemaker.

"You've been awfully quiet today." Grandmother gave her a sideways glance. "I didn't mean to upset you last night, but I didn't know an easy way to tell you what Thaniel and I hypothesized. And it is just a hypothesis at this point."

"You and Jacob seem pretty convinced."

"So is Thaniel, to be honest."

Sarah's gaze dropped to the dirty water trickling between the cobblestones. If Deborah's disturbing prophecy one day came to pass, the streets of the holy city would flow with white fire. What would that bizarre event mean for the people walking these streets then and now? Would she even live to see that day? If so, what would that time be like for her and Jacob and, most importantly, their son?

All around her, the city's oblivious residents went about their work or errands, or enjoyed an early dinner with friends. "Why can I never seem to have what they have?"

Grandmother turned to her. "What do you mean?"

"An ordinary life in an ordinary time. Or at least what appears to be an ordinary time."

"The end of the age has to come for some generation, and we don't get to choose when." She slowed her brisk pace. "You've been given an extraordinary gift, as has Jacob. They are not meant to go to waste."

"I know." Sarah dropped her voice. "But if it's true about the Heir, I should feel honored and excited, grateful even. But right now, I'm mostly afraid."

"I confess I'm a little fearful too." Grandmother adjusted her scarf as the mist became a steady drizzle. "But just because we don't know what the future holds, that doesn't mean we won't be ready when it arrives."

Sarah lifted the hood of her cloak, although wet hair didn't rate highly on her list of concerns. Maybe it would be decades before the end of the age arrived, and she would be ready by then.

A few minutes later, she removed a scrap of paper from her pocket and rechecked the address of the house for rent. "We're almost there. It should be around this corner and half a block down."

Grandmother paused across from a rundown tavern. "This neighborhood leaves much to be desired."

Sarah stepped over the soggy leaves that littered the gutter, and Grandmother followed her across the street.

"Do you smell that?" The wind must have shifted because Sarah caught a whiff of something rotten.

Grandmother waved a hand in front of her nose. "I think I should give you a pay raise."

"I hope it's better farther down the street." The stink threatened to bring back the nausea Sarah thought she'd left behind a month ago.

Unconvinced, Grandmother stopped in front of a section of wall plastered with notices of rooms and houses for rent. "Maybe we can find something in a less unsavory area."

Sarah had wandered a short way down the street when door bells jingled nearby. A girl of eight or nine came out and sat on the damp stoop.

A wooden sign creaked on its rusty chain above the girl's curly head. Something seemed familiar about the sign with a bright red, blue, and gold card painted on it. Sarah pulled her cloak tighter against the growing chill. She was sure she'd never been down this street before.

Her tangled curls bouncing, the little girl waved to her. "Come here."

Sarah walked over to her. "Hello."

Door bells jangled again, and a woman with the same dark curls and rounded face stuck her head out the door. "Get back in here," she yelled. "We have a customer."

A pulse of anger passed over Sarah, and she rubbed her temple.

"When is a blessing a curse and a curse a blessing?" The little girl giggled.

She leaned over. "I don't think I know that riddle."

"Are you sure?" asked the girl in a singsong voice.

The foul-smelling dampness pressed in on Sarah, and her stomach roiled at an unseen darkness nearby. She glanced at the doorway behind the girl, but her mother had vanished.

"I'll tell you the answer, but it's a secret," the girl stepped closer. "He who sleeps beneath the earth cursed us to guard against the dreaded birth."

Sarah recoiled. "What did you say?"

The girl's eyes clouded, then dropped to Sarah's midsection. "I will tell you a fortune most foul because I know what you carry," came the deep voice of a man. "It shall be a curse to you, and the price you pay will be death."

"No." Bile rose in Sarah's throat as she staggered backward.

The girl's mouth contorted into a sneer as she reached out her hand to Sarah. "You must pay."

The woman reappeared on the top step, her hands on her ample hips. "Hey, if she told your fortune, you need to pay. We don't work for free here."

A firm hand clamped onto Sarah's shoulder from behind. "What's going on?" Grandmother asked.

"Demon," she choked out a whisper. "In the little girl."

"We need to go now." Grandmother pulled her across the street as a man came out of the shop, his shirt untucked and a bottle in his hand.

The woman scowled. "They didn't pay."

"You gonna stiff a little girl?" The man loped down the short flight of steps. "You look like you can afford it."

"Keep your face covered," Grandmother urged as they hurried down the street.

"When is a blessing a curse and a curse a blessing?" The demon child cackled.

"Come back," her mother called. "We're just trying to put food on the table for our little girl."

Strangers turned to stare.

Sarah looked over her shoulder as the man broke into a trot.

The demon shook a puny fist from the doorstep. "You will pay," it screeched.

Several unkempt men loitering outside the tavern joined in the pursuit, parroting calls of "you need to pay."

Grandmother tugged on Sarah's cloak, and they turned down a side street as fast as her rubbery legs could carry her. The men continued their shouted accusations, but thankfully the demon's screams could no longer reach them.

The men were gaining ground as they headed toward a busy market a block away. Grandmother must be planning to escape into the crowd, then find a carriage for hire to take them home.

Instead, she swerved into a narrow alley.

Sarah rounded the corner behind her and slid to a stop, a brick wall twenty yards ahead. "It's a dead end."

13

THE HIDDEN PERSON

Sarah whirled around. "They're coming. We've got to get out of here."

But Grandmother was counting the doors in the muddy alley. "Here…" She reached for the handle and shoved the door open. "Thank heaven," she whispered as she pulled Sarah inside and bolted the door.

She held a finger to her lips while Sarah pressed her ear to the door, her legs shaking as if they would rather her keep running.

Outside, the sporadic shouts faded. Either their pursuers were well past, or their zeal had faded. Sarah looked around the dim storeroom with spools of yarn on wide shelves and rolled-up rugs leaning against the wall. A light shone from a room in front that looked out on the street. Grandmother sat down at the small desk in the corner and helped herself to pen and paper.

"What is this place?" Sarah whispered.

"It's my rug making business. We employ some of the women we've rescued from slavery here." Grandmother dipped her pen in a small inkwell and began to write. "The ones who can safely remain in the city, that is."

This small sanctuary in a rough neighborhood bore her grandmother's penchant for order and cleanliness.

Sarah listened at the door again just in case their pursuers decided to backtrack in search of them. But all she could hear was Grandmother's pen scratching on her paper...until soft footsteps sounded behind them.

A thin young woman pulled up short with a squeal. "Oh, Madam Magdala. I'm so sorry. I was just coming to lock the door."

"It's quite all right, Hildah."

"We're closing up for the day, but how may I help you?"

"My...assistant and I were in the vicinity, and I thought I'd see about the sales figures for the month."

"Yes, of course." She gestured toward a black ledger on a shelf above the desk.

"On your way home, would you please deliver this note." Grandmother dipped her pen in ink again and scrawled an address on the envelope. "It's a matter of urgency."

"Certainly, Madam Magdala."

"Oh, and there seems to have been some sort of disturbance a few blocks over," Grandmother added. "So be careful leaving, and be sure to lock the door behind you."

"Yes, ma'am." Hildah retreated with the note.

Sarah watched from the storeroom as the young woman walked with a slight limp past several looms and a stack of rugs, then out the front door.

"What do we do now?" She asked when Hildah shut the door behind her and turned the key in the lock.

"We wait for Goran to fetch us." Grandmother propped her elbow on the small desk and massaged her temple.

Sarah sank onto an overturned crate and rested her hand on her soft belly. "How did it know about me and the baby?"

"Unfortunately, demons can see the truth... They don't like it, but they recognize it. Then they'll do everything in their power to pervert it and subvert it if it suits their wicked purposes."

Sarah sighed. "How did I not realize that girl had a demon?"

"Demons are nothing if not crafty."

"I sensed something dark nearby, but I was completely fooled. I assumed it was the mother."

Grandmother scooted her chair closer. "You're being too hard on yourself."

"I don't think so since I just ran from a child."

"No, we ran from a dark spirit, and it was the right thing to do under the circumstances."

"Clearly I'm not ready for this." Sarah's eyes stung. "Am I just supposed to hide my whole life?"

"Remember, we are the faithful remnant and we are far from powerless. We have the living God on our side and his Sacred Fire burning within us."

"I know that, but how am I supposed to protect my baby? I can barely protect myself."

"For one thing, we now know this is not the neighborhood for you," Grandmother said with a wry smile. "But I trust the Fourth Scroll will have answers for us, and Reliqui Fideles will help keep you safe."

Sarah shook her head. "Matthias will never believe I'm the mother of the Heir, when he doesn't even think I'm good enough for his son. Honestly, some days I'm not even sure I'm good enough for Jacob, let alone be the mother of the lord and priest of the everlasting age."

Grandmother reached for her hand and gave it a gentle squeeze. "When I was a young woman, about five years older than you are now, I met your grandfather for the first time. My mother had recently died, and my father remarried soon after."

Sarah leaned against the wall. If Grandmother's story was meant to be comforting, it sure wasn't starting out that way.

"My new stepmother made clear she had little regard for me and encouraged my father to marry me off as soon as possible. She wanted her son to inherit my father's small trading company in Midiah. But I was stubborn, and my father didn't want to saddle me with a cruel husband."

Sarah had heard little about her grandmother's early years, but it seemed they'd involved more hardship than she'd assumed. Grandmother also faced the pain of rejection in the midst of grief and upheaval.

"Bartholomew was twelve years older than me, but he was kind and wise, and he admired my ability to do sums in my head. When he asked me to marry him and move to the holy city, I was surprised. But seeing no future for myself in Midiah, I agreed."

Her finger brushed her silver wedding band. "Your grandfather saw something in me at that young age that I didn't see in myself. He taught me much about the business of the House of Magdala, of course. But even more so, he taught me how to overcome challenges and to forge alliances."

The alliance of Reliqui Fideles had come to the aid of Sarah and Jonah in times of dire need. Her heart warmed as she looked around the modest business her grandmother had built to give women like Hildah freedom and a new start in life.

"Since Bartholomew had no siblings, I had to take over more of the business when his health began to fail. By the time you were born, his heart was giving him trouble, and he had frequent spells when he couldn't work."

Grandmother smiled, her eyes distant. "My goodness, he doted on you. He would sit in the kitchen with you in his lap while Rebecca and Marta baked bread. He swore your presence brought him peace. I didn't think much of it at the time, just that he loved you. But now I wonder if he saw you for the peacemaker you were prophesied to become. And I just dismissed it as the sentiment of a loving grandfather.

"But now you've come back to me, and I can see the hidden person of the heart, and I think the living God has chosen most wisely."

GORAN'S CARRIAGE rolled through the dark city streets at a leisurely pace so as not to draw unwanted attention. They neared a street lamp, and light shone on Grandmother's taut face as she stared out the window. No doubt her keen mind mulled their next steps.

Sarah leaned back on the leather seat, concealed in the shadows. At the moment, she didn't want to think about the demonic forces arrayed against them, and necessary plans to counter them. She just wanted to get home to her husband who also saw the hidden person of her heart and loved her unconditionally. And he must've been worried sick by their absence.

After whispering words of thanks to Goran, they slipped out of the carriage and through the front door.

Jacob and George rushed down the hall, with Marta trailing after them.

"Where have you been?" Jacob reached for Sarah.

"You're almost two hours late for dinner." Marta patted her chest. "We were getting so worried."

"With good reason." Grandmother pushed past them into the parlor, then peered through the curtains at the street. "I don't believe we were followed."

Jacob's brown eyes widened. "Followed?"

"What happened?" George asked.

Sarah took a deep breath. "We went to look at that apartment for let, and this little girl began talking to me. I thought she was harmless, but she had a demon." Her voice broke. "It knows about the baby, the Heir. It said horrible, vile things."

Jacob tensed beside her.

"Then we were chased down the street with taunts and threats," Grandmother added.

George snarled. "It chased you?"

"Not the demon child, just her drunken father and other troublemakers." Grandmother yanked off her wet scarf. "We had to hide in the rug shop until Goran got my message and came to fetch us."

Sarah turned to Marta with a sudden jolt of recognition. "The eye on the fortuneteller's sign...her symbol was similar to the necklace the palm reader wore."

"The slitted green eye? Well, that's odd."

"What palm reader?" Grandmother asked.

"It was while Jacob was away." Marta wrung her hands. "Poor Sarah was so despondent I thought a walk in the sunshine would do her good."

Jacob cringed and held her tighter.

George's eyebrows shot up. "You took her to a palm reader?"

"Heavens no! I was delivering a message for Demetrius, and things were going fine until this frizzy haired diviner took an interest in Sarah. What was it she said? Something about your aura?"

"She said I had a peaceful aura, and she wanted to read my lines." Sarah held up her hand. "But I wouldn't let her. Then she got really mad and grabbed my wrist. There was such darkness within her, I kind of felt sorry for her. I tried to help her, to give her a few moments of peace. But that just seemed to make her even more angry." She rubbed her wrist. "That's when Marta found me.

Grandmother's stony expression led Marta to back up a step. "Why am I just hearing about this?"

"It didn't seem that important at the time," she said sheepishly.

"It certainly appears so now."

George rubbed his bald head. "What are we going to do about this situation?"

"That dark spirit knows way too much," Jacob said as the bells sounded for evening prayers. "We're going to need Peter."

14

MIDNIGHT MISSION

Thanks to Jacob's censer, a dense fog obscured the alley behind the fortuneteller's house. Faint firelight flickered in the upstairs window where the demon-possessed girl should be asleep by now. A few blocks away, Goran waited with his carriage to return him, along with Peter and George, to the bakery.

A black garbed figure strode through the fog. "The parents have been in the tavern for over an hour now, drinking pretty heavily," George reported.

"Good." Peter turned to Garth. "You're up."

Jacob uncorked a small jug and handed it to him.

Garth poured some of the ale into his cupped hand, then splashed it on his beard and the front of his shirt. "Now I'll fit right in."

"Careful," Jacob said. "That's infused with sleeping incense, and a pinch of my secret ingredient for memory loss."

"George, as soon as Garth knows who to target, come back to guard the alley for us," Peter instructed. "Then we can get this nasty business over with."

"Good luck," Jacob whispered as the two men disappeared in the fog.

Peter studied the rickety staircase leading to the second story apartment. "We really need to train some students to handle these midnight missions. I should be in my own bed at this hour."

"You don't believe me, do you?" asked Jacob now that they were alone.

Peter crossed his arms. "What?"

"About our baby being the Heir."

"Well, there is one glaring problem with your theory."

Only one? Jacob thought Peter would come up with several, at a minimum. "What would that be?"

"If the Heir to the Sacred Fire is coming soon, it seems like he would be my son, not yours."

"True, but things don't always turn out as it seems they should." Jacob tried to gauge his brother's expression through the wispy fog. "Maybe you and Cecilia will have lots of girls."

"Or maybe that demon was spewing lies to torment Sarah."

"Hannah and Thaniel were convinced even before this incident."

"People have been convinced of the Heir's imminent arrival for centuries...and been wrong." Peter shrugged. "Just the same, I'll not have Sarah or any future niece or nephew of mine threatened by a dark spirit."

"That's generous of you." Jacob waved his fogging censer to add to their cover. Then he traded it for the censer with sleeping incense that hung from the branch of a spindly tree.

"Put it to sleep if things get dangerous." Peter eyed the demon's abode. "But let's see if we can get some useful information first."

George materialized again. "The parents should be passed out cold within ten minutes."

"Hopefully they won't have any idea what happened." Peter

moved toward the wooden staircase. "Stay down here. I don't think these steps will hold you."

"This is going to be delicate handling a child," Jacob whispered as they headed up. "Are you sure you can do it?"

"I'll do my part. Just make sure you do yours." Peter reached for the handle, glancing sideways at Jacob. His expression shifted to surprise. "It's unlocked."

The door creaked open. The smell of rotting food and human waste greeted them.

Peter shook his head. "Just look at this filth."

As if waiting for them, a dark-haired girl sat on a small pallet on the floor. "Are you here to help me?"

Jacob nodded. "In a manner of speaking, yes."

The girl tucked her knees to her chest. "He won't like that."

Peter leaned over. "Who won't?"

The girl raised a grimy hand, her finger pointing at the ceiling. "Him."

Peter straightened and slowly turned in a complete circle. "This girl is not possessed."

"What? Then who?" Jacob jerked his head toward the door. "The mother?"

"No, but it's here somewhere." Peter's gaze took in the room. "The dark spirit that speaks through them."

"He doesn't want you here." The girl began to rock on the floor. "He hates priests."

"Not surprising in the least." Peter looked up at the soot-stained ceiling. "What is his name?"

The girl twitched, her face scrunching and reddening.

Jacob tensed as Peter reached in his pocket for a vial of holy water. "I speak to the dark spirit. What is your name?"

The child's lips pulled back over her teeth. "So it is true about the girl." The gravelly voice of a man passed unnaturally through her lips. "You would not have come otherwise."

"In the name of the living God, what is your name, demon?"

"Sharar." It replied with a hiss that made the hairs on the back of Jacob's neck stand up. "You can't find all of us, priest. The Seer's eyes are many, watching for her, the harbinger of peace." The girl's dry lips twisted into a sickening sneer. "A peace that will never come because we will rip the child from her womb and devour it."

"No!" Jacob leapt forward.

"Then Arxmeus will rise again."

"That's a lie." Jacob's fist clenched.

"Kadmiel's temple will be reborn on the rubble of your precious cathedral," the demon spat.

"Stay back, Jacob." Peter stiff-armed him. "It's baiting you. It knows its time here is up, and it would like nothing better than to make you into a murderer before we're done tonight."

"A new age of Arxmeus is upon us," the demon hissed.

"In the name of the living God, shut up," Peter commanded.

Its lips moved silently, tongue flapping in agitation.

"That's better," Peter said. "Now, Sharar, you will leave this child and never oppress or possess her again, in the name of the living God."

As he sprinkled the girl with holy water, her face slackened, and she blinked at them with relief. Then, with a whimper, she scrambled under the kitchen table.

"Now where is it?" Jacob whirled around.

"It's still here, although it would like us to believe otherwise." Peter scanned the items strewn around the room. "It must be bound to an object. Look for something a dark spirit could be connected to."

Jacob rifled through a trunk of moldy clothes and blankets in the corner. "What exactly am I looking for?"

"I don't know." As Peter lifted the corner of a lumpy mattress on the floor, a candle holder flew by his head. "Watch out!"

A tin cup grazed Jacob's shoulder as he moved toward the shelves on the wall.

Covering her ears, the girl curled into a ball under the wooden table.

Shelves shook. Jacob ducked as a heavy goblet hurtled toward him. Peter opened a kitchen cabinet, and a plate flew past his face and smashed against the far wall.

"We must be getting closer," Peter called over the din.

Something gleamed on the highest shelf. Dust rose, and the shelves buckled as Jacob reached for a polished wooden container, gold around the edges. A blue slitted eye surrounded by a crescent moon and stars adorned the lid.

"Over here." Jacob lifted the lid a fraction of an inch. "Cards...demonic cards!"

"That's it." His brother leapt to his side. "Close it now."

Cards flapped frantically inside the shiny box.

"You're going into the vault for all eternity." Peter clamped his hand on top of the cursed object. "In the name of the living God, I seal this box with the Sacred Fire that burns within me."

The edges glowed white, then faded.

Jacob stared at the box, now a demonic tomb. But how many more dark spirits lurking in the holy city knew, or suspected, the same as Sharar?

"You two all right?" George shouted through a broken window.

"Yeah, but we'd better get out of here." Peter grabbed the box and headed for the door. "The whole neighborhood probably heard this racket."

Jacob snatched his censer from the table.

He crouched down and whispered to the huddled girl, "It's gone, and it's not coming back." Although he wished he could say the same about her loathsome parents.

As she nodded, tendrils of silver incense wafted toward her. Her eyelids fluttered closed, and she rolled onto her side.

"Sweet dreams, and may the living God watch over you."

Jacob turned and followed after his elder brother who stomped down the stairs. Thankfully Peter was gifted in spiritual battle, but his ego must have suffered a serious blow. He had to know that if Sarah were pregnant with the Heir to the Sacred Fire, then he would be the last High Priest of Aclesia, potentially bypassing Peter in the line of succession.

Recalling their dying mother's prophecy and the nightmare that still haunted his sleep, Jacob contemplated an even worse outcome for his brother...and himself.

15

MEETING OF THE REMNANT

S arah scanned the sidewalk ahead as she and Grandmother walked along the wide boulevard that ran through the center of the holy city. She'd been surprised when Grandmother invited her to visit Garth and his wife, Clara. Since the encounter several weeks ago with the demon child, she'd not ventured far from the bakery or cathedral. But any chance to see family was a welcome comfort, and maybe the safety and anonymity of the crowded thoroughfare put Grandmother's mind at ease.

Her scarf covered her gray hair and much of her face despite the mild fall day with little wind. Sarah glanced over her shoulder. About twenty yards back, a heavyset man in a drab brown jacket wore his wide-brimmed hat tilted down so she couldn't make out his face. Wasn't he the same man who'd rushed in front of an approaching carriage to cross the street near them a few blocks back, earning a rebuke from the driver?

As they turned off the bustling main thoroughfare, she caught another glimpse of the large figure behind a group of tradesmen. Pausing, she pretended to look in the window of a dress shop as he hastened around the corner. He stumbled to a stop, then reached into his pocket for his watch, as if he suddenly needed to check the time.

In two quick strides, Sarah caught up to Grandmother and whispered, "Why is George following us?"

Without slowing her pace, she replied, "Because I asked him to, although it seems he's not up to his usual standard of stealth today."

They headed down another side street and soon entered Clara's front garden. George ambled past, appearing in no hurry to reach his destination.

"Where's he going?" Sarah asked.

Grandmother reached for the iron knocker. "Oh, he'll be joining us shortly."

Clara opened the door and quickly ushered them into the foyer. After pecking them both on the cheek and exchanging greetings, she gestured to the doorway of a spacious parlor with high ceilings and dark wood paneled walls. A fire blazed in the hearth, and candles in wall sconces lined the room. Sarah crinkled her nose at the faint scent of pipe smoke.

"How you doing, sweetheart?" Her father's cousin Garth gave her a one-armed squeeze before turning to Grandmother. "Any trouble on the way over?"

"None, as far as I could tell." She headed for a blue armchair closest to the fireplace.

A middle-aged man with short, dark hair and a neatly trimmed beard stood against the wall facing the door. "Hello, Sarah."

She looked again at the man and his military bearing. She'd met him briefly on her arrival to the holy city but mainly knew him by reputation. "Captain?"

He nodded. "You can call me Demetrius."

A pang of grief struck Sarah in this manly room with her late father's best friend, Demetrius, and cousin Garth. She pictured a forty-year-old version of Jonah propping his feet up on the chinked wooden table in front of the sofa, laughing in the company of his closest companions.

She took a seat at the end of the sofa, near the only other person in the room remotely her age. A willowy young woman with straight dark hair smiled at her from a large stuffed chair that seemed like it could swallow her up.

"This is Fiona." Demetrius looked down at her, the hard angles of his face softening.

"Nice to meet—"

A faint floral scent wafted through the stale smoke.

"You're the flower seller from the market." Sarah rubbed her wrist, recalling that strange afternoon and the palm reader's foul grip.

"I am."

The fine lines around the corners of her eyes and mouth suggested Fiona was older than she appeared from a distance. Probably in her mid-thirties, if Sarah had to guess.

Garth sat down next to her, the springs of the sofa groaning in protest. Soon his older brother Goran entered the room with George in tow. They must have cut through the backyard from Goran's house and workshop next door.

"Good, we're all here." Grandmother nodded in satisfaction.

"This is risky for us to be together." Goran moved to the window, pulling back the curtain a couple inches to peer out at the street.

Demetrius crossed his arms over his broad chest. "Yes, next time let's invite the high priest to draw a little more attention."

Grandmother pursed her lips. "I wouldn't have called this meeting had I not thought it absolutely necessary."

Clara set a cup of tea on the small round table at her side. "Anyone else care for tea?"

Given the sudden tension in the room, Sarah and the rest declined. Clara sat down on the other side of her husband, and all eyes turned toward Grandmother.

"Thank you for coming." She looked around the room at Reliqui Fideles in the flesh. "It's far too difficult and dangerous to correspond via letter about such a complicated and sensitive subject."

"I don't mean to spoil the party," Demetrius said, "but how can we be sure Sarah's carrying the Heir to the Sacred Fire?" His eyes went to her midsection. "It seems too preposterous to be true... No offense, Sarah."

Garth chuckled. "I can only imagine what Thaddeus would have to say about the Heir being a blood relative of ours."

His brother Goran's expression turned serious. "What does Matthias think about all this?"

"He's not yet convinced," Grandmother replied. "But Thaniel makes a very compelling case that all the prophecies and signs are converging—"

"Wait, Matthias doesn't even believe it." Goran rubbed the bridge of his nose. "Is Thaniel really a greater authority than the high priest?"

"He's a more open minded one, that's for certain." Grandmother's face twisted into a frown. "That stubborn old goat still hasn't forgiven Jacob and Sarah for marrying without his knowledge and approval."

Sarah had to smile at the pulse of righteous anger from her loving grandmother.

"I think we can all agree there's something about Sarah the dark spirits are strongly opposed to," George said from the hearth. "The versarius wouldn't have targeted her otherwise."

"But the truth is, we can't know for sure at the moment." Grandmother reached for her tea cup. "Only time will tell."

"Yes, it will." Demetrius said. "You can only keep a pregnancy hidden for so long."

Sarah rested her hand on her rounded belly and the new life inside her, already part of this gathering of the faithful remnant, contentious though it may be.

"Maybe folks will just assume you've been eating too much bread." Garth winked at her.

Clara shook her head. "Oh, hush."

"Look, we're wasting time." Demetrius stood at attention. "What do we know so far, and what do we need to do going forward?"

Grandmother waved a bony hand. "We need to know who these fortunetellers are and why they're here. And specifically, what do they know about Sarah, and how big of a threat do they pose? Fiona, what can you tell us about the palm reader?"

"I remember her setting up shop last spring. She sells her crystals mainly, and she seems to have built a steady business. She rarely interacts with any of the other merchants or draws attention to herself."

"Continue to keep a close eye on her," Grandmother advised. "Clara, what do you have to report?"

Sarah leaned around Garth. So Clara, the picture of a middle-aged homemaker, was engaged in clandestine activities too.

"I watched her several times at the market, and even trailed her home once, but I didn't notice anything suspicious. She lives alone in a one-bedroom apartment in the tavern district."

"Do you remember her wearing a necklace with a green cat's eye?" Sarah asked.

Clara drew in a breath. "Yes, there was a green slitted eye. And I noticed her heavy gold chain, which seemed expensive for one who lived so modestly."

"That symbol on her necklace was similar to the sign above the fortuneteller's place," Sarah said. "It showed a red card with a blue slitted eye surrounded by gold stars. Not exactly the same, but I think it means something important."

A vein pulsed in Demetrius's temple. "I saw a symbol like that at another soothsayer's booth near the garrison. Come to think of it, she hasn't been around long either." He rubbed his beard. "Unfortunately, there's been a long line of soldiers waiting for their fortunes to be told on a number of occasions."

"Not a wise way to spend one's hard-earned coin," George said.

"No..." Demetrius shook his head. "And some of the boys are far too gullible."

"She'll tell the young men what she thinks they want to hear to gain their trust, and that can open a door to any number of dark spirits," Fiona said ominously.

"And their lies." Goran peeked through the curtain again. "That's how they operate."

Fiona gave a regretful nod. "Fortunetellers will spread their lies, especially if they believe them to be true."

"How do you know so much about fortune tellers?" Sarah asked.

Her gaze fell to the rug. "Because I used to be one."

"Oh." Sarah's eyes widened, but the only darkness emanating from Fiona seemed to be shame.

Silence hung heavy until Garth said, "But then you saw the light, huh Fi?"

Her eyes went to the flames licking the dry logs in the fireplace. "Yes, thankfully."

"All right then." Grandmother returned her tea cup to its saucer. "There certainly appears to be a connection between these fortunetellers, but might there be others too?"

"I'll check the soothsayer's booth later, but we should all keep a lookout for that symbol." Demetrius shifted his weight as if ready to dart off and attend to his task.

Grandmother looked up at George resting his huge hand on the fireplace mantel. "What else have you learned about the tarot card reader and her hideous cackling fiend?"

At the mention of the demon, Sarah's stomach churned, and its evil assertions echoed in her mind. *You will pay...and the price will be death.*

George straightened. "Her husband's a drunk who works at the tavern next door, and she occasionally waits tables. Apparently, she's been reading cards for years, but recently something happened that's proven more lucrative for her."

"Yeah, she bragged about that after a few tankards of ale," Garth said. "But I couldn't make any sense of it, what with all her slurring and nonsense about cards and signs."

"But what would have changed?" Sarah asked.

"Don't know, but I'd rather not go back to find out," George said. "Drunk as those two were, I don't think they'd recognize me, but there's something creepy about the place."

Grandmother gripped the arms of her chair. "No, you and Garth must stay away from there. We don't want to tip our hand. What concerns me most though, is who else knows what it surmised?"

"Or alleged," Goran said. "We can't assume it was telling the truth."

"No, we shouldn't assume anything when it comes to dark spirits," Demetrius said.

"They know things...unseen things," Fiona murmured.

"At least we got to it within hours of it confronting Sarah," George said.

Grandmother nodded. "But could it have communicated with other demons or fortunetellers in that time?"

"Possibly." George ran a hand over his bald head. "That was no lesser demon."

"Yeah, it made quite a ruckus for the priests." Garth glanced at George. "We've faced worse, but it was a powerful one."

Sarah shuddered. Jacob had been short on details, just suggesting that Peter took care of the situation with minimal assistance needed from the rest of them. She turned to Fiona. "Jacob said the dark spirit mentioned a Seer. Do you know anything about that?"

Fiona went rigid. "The Seer?"

All eyes darted to the former fortuneteller.

"I've only heard vague rumors…"

Based on the tremor in Fiona's voice, Sarah wasn't sure she wanted to know more.

"The Seer's supposedly a powerful medium, gifted in all forms of divination…astrology, tarot cards, palm reading, crystals, curses, and so forth."

Faces paled around the room.

"But I don't know if it's a dark spirit, an actual person, or just a legend."

Sarah bit her lip, hoping for the latter.

"Whoever, or whatever, the Seer may be," Demetrius said, "I fear the recent actions of the priests will not go unanswered."

"Unfortunately, you're right to do so." Fiona twisted her slender hands.

Grandmother let out a deep sigh. "Then we must be on our guard as we await their next move."

As to what form that next move would take, Sarah didn't have a clue. The only thing she was sure of was that it could be deadly.

16

THE WHITE THEOPHANY

The bed creaked as Jacob stirred in his sleep. Sarah snuggled against him to stay warm in the pre-dawn chill.

"No, father," he mumbled. "I'm not…"

Sarah shook him gently. "You're dreaming."

He rolled onto his back and ran his fingers through his tousled hair. "Sorry if I woke you."

"You were having that dream again."

He reached his arm around Sarah and pulled her closer. "It's nothing."

She rested her head on his chest. His rapidly beating heart suggested otherwise. "This dream's been bothering you for months."

She'd assumed it had to do with his strained relationship with his father over their marriage, but another possibility made her own heart race. Was he worried about their baby or becoming a father?

"I need to get dressed." He slipped out of bed in the faint moonlight. "You should rest a little longer."

"Does it have to do with the baby?"

"No." He yanked on his shirt.

She propped herself on her elbow. "Remember that day in the apple orchard when you asked me to marry you?"

He froze. "Yes."

"You said there should be no more secrets between us."

"It's just a fading dream that doesn't mean anything." He grabbed his robe hanging over a chair and started toward the door. "I'll see you at the Awakening service."

"Yes...the Awakening." Sarah pulled the quilt up to her chin, but the lingering warmth offered no comfort. Soon she would trudge through the damp cold to sit in the dark cathedral where her grandmother would pretend she was her servant, and her husband would pretend he barely knew her. As for her father-in-law, the high priest, he probably wished she'd never been born.

About ten minutes later, she heard Marta and George banging about the kitchen. Since the first of the three holy days was a time of fasting and repentance, there would be no breakfast. Tea was all they could look forward to until dinner time.

But when Sarah entered the kitchen, Marta had tea along with a plate with bread and cheese waiting for her.

"Pregnant women aren't subject to the fast." Grandmother motioned for her to join her at the table.

Sarah slumped onto a chair and wrapped her hands around her tea cup, the steam hot on her face. "I'm really not hungry."

Grandmother, Marta, and George flanked Sarah as they entered the cathedral, not fearing for her safety, but in case anyone looked too closely. At five months pregnant, the heavy wool cloak helped conceal Sarah's condition, but for how much longer?

A short while later, the choir began their low chant of

lament, and the priests processed into the dim nave. Jacob's tired eyes flitted in her direction. Should she bring up his troubling dreams later? Or heed her grandmother's advice that they would go away in time, and just let it go? Either way, she was left with a hollow ache in her chest.

When the choir finished, Peter made his way forward. Just as he commenced a somber prayer in the forgotten language, a strong draft of wind rattled the windows and set the small candles in the wall sconces sputtering. Sarah breathed deeply of the unusual scent from his smoking silver censer. The hint of fresh pine reminded her of winter in the mountains. She lifted her gaze to the stained-glass scene of snow-capped Mount Peniel. Its winding path ended with an ancient exhortation to walk the path of faith to find the desires of your heart. She let out a long sigh. But what did the path of faith look like for her and Jacob now, and where might it take them?

Peter concluded his prayer with *in nominees de Vivendi*, and the high priest rose and ascended to his lectern.

"Hearken unto me, all ye faithful," he began. "At the dawn of this second age, the faithful and their wayward brethren awoke to the fruits of rebellion...the city on the hill laid waste, the temple of Arxmeus a smoldering ruin..."

A shiver passed through Sarah. Thousands of years ago, the once-great city of Arxmeus had become an abomination, its temple utterly destroyed in the cataclysmic battle between Lord Kadmiel and Lord Uriel. Yet the fortunetelling demon claimed to Jacob and Peter that Arxmeus would rise again on this same holy ground.

"But from the mines of Machaerus in the north to the groves of Midiah in the south, the bondage of the faithful had ended," the high priest's voice thundered. "At first light, their chains fell away, as broken as the earth from which they were formed."

Behind him loomed the stained-glass of a priest reaching

for the Fourth Scroll but not quite touching it. The mysterious scroll gleamed white at this frosty daybreak. Did it hold the answers they sought? Is that why the crystal cabinet appeared to her when Jacob took her to visit the secret Scroll Room last fall? Sarah leaned back on the hard wooden pew, tired in body and spirit. But she promised herself and Grandmother that she wouldn't fall asleep during the service again this year.

"On the High Plain of Nirel, a new light beckoned!" Matthias proclaimed. "From the staff of Uriel, a white fire shone through the darkness, calling the remnant to return. For at the end of those dark years, the living God opened his heavenly storehouses in blessing, and there was a sowing of peace throughout the land.

A sowing of peace? It seemed as if the faithful had held their collective breath, waiting in the cold for that precious glimmer of hope. A peace not of her own making settled over Sarah, and a heavy weight slipped from her shoulders.

Matthias descended from his pulpit. Jacob and Peter rose to stand on either side of their father. At the end of the somber Awakening, there would be no blessing of bread, nor anointing with the Sacred Fire. Instead the high priest lifted his hands. "Remember...what was once squandered and lost will one day be redeemed and restored."

Sarah stood with the others to depart, less burdened for herself as a peacemaker and for the prophesied baby growing in her womb. For at the end of this age, there would come another sowing of peace, an everlasting one.

The faithful began to exit through the bronze doors at the rear. A sudden shriek halted the shuffling footsteps and hushed conversations.

Grandmother clamped her hand on Sarah's forearm and whispered, "Wait."

George leapt into the aisle and pushed through the crowd. More shouts echoed from the entry way. Peter shouldered his way forward with Jacob close behind. Jacob glanced at Sarah as he passed, his brow knitted with worry and regret.

She stood on her tiptoes as the three of them disappeared into the chaotic entry. Quieting her mind, her awareness spread outward, but she couldn't detect anything hostile amid the mass of confusion that permeated the nave.

A few moments later, George reappeared and motioned them forward, a huge grin on his face.

Outside, thick snowflakes fell from the sky, coating the holy city in a blanket of white. Young kids, dragged from their warm beds an hour ago, ran through the two-inch-deep snow, whooping and sliding on the cobblestones.

Jacob stood at the bottom of the steps, his arms outstretched as snowflakes settled on his dark hair and robe. His eyes found Sarah's, and his mouth formed a crooked smile...until a snowball exploded on the side of his head.

Near the arcade, Peter howled with laughter.

Shaking the snow off his head, Jacob scooped up a handful of snow and charged after his brother.

Peter ducked behind a cluster of elderly women, their faces crinkled with delight in the white morning. Then he snaked through the chattering crowd and doubled back toward the cathedral. But before he could find sanctuary, Sarah's snowball caught him square in the chest, spraying snow on his neck and face.

Peter skidded to a stop, wiping wet snow from his reddened cheeks.

"He wouldn't hit a pregnant woman, would he?" Marta whispered as he packed more snow into a ball.

Sarah stepped behind George, just in case.

IN THE EVENING light of the winter solstice, Sarah sat at the kitchen table watching the remaining snowflakes drift down from the silver-tinged sky.

"Aren't you the lucky one?" Marta set a plate of cold chicken, a slab of cheese, and bread in front of her.

Jacob carried bowls of vegetable soup to the table. She'd get to indulge while the rest of them ate the meager Awakening meal of thin soup, nuts, and dried fruit.

"This hardly seems fair," Sarah said.

"Who said anything about fair?" Marta added another slice of bread to Sarah's plate. "Since you're eating for two…"

"Enjoy it, both of you." Jacob grinned and raised his glass of water to her.

George tore his envious gaze away from Sarah's plate. "I bet the snow will be gone tomorrow, as soon as the wind shifts from the west."

"But my goodness, it sure is beautiful." Marta took her seat.

"In my forty years in the holy city, I don't ever remember it snowing here." Grandmother reached for her napkin. "In the foothills and the villages to the north, certainly, but not here."

"You couldn't ask for more perfect timing." George started on his soup.

"Indeed." Grandmother turned to Jacob. "Might it be a heavenly portent?"

"I thought the same," he said.

"Seems to be a lot of those lately," Marta said.

"For those who care to see to them." Grandmother shifted on her chair. "Jacob, under what circumstances should the Fourth Scroll be opened?"

"We don't really know." He reached for his spoon. "The only stipulation I'm aware of, is that it must be opened and read by the high priest. Unfortunately, only he can break the silver seal."

Grandmother pursed her lips. "Seeing as we are at his mercy, what does your father think of recent developments?"

"The few times I've tried to talk to him, he brushes me off or changes the subject. At the moment, he seems more focused on announcing Peter's engagement to Cecilia and introducing her and her family to the other First Families when they come for the Calling in a couple months."

And Sarah suspected the high priest wasn't happy about the extra complications her pregnancy presented, even if he didn't believe their baby was the prophesied Heir to the Sacred Fire.

Her grandmother glanced at the clock in the corner as it struck the hour. "I may need to have another talk with your father, because events are underway that are well beyond our control and understanding." She cleared her throat. "It may not be safe for Sarah to remain in the holy city for much longer."

Sarah's eyes widened. "What?"

Jacob tensed, his spoon scraping his empty bowl. "But I can't be separated from Sarah and our baby, and I can't abandon my father and Peter."

Marta's rosy cheeks paled. "Surely she and the baby would be safe here."

George ran a hand over his bald head. "I'll see to that myself."

"I don't want to leave the holy city ever again." Sarah's chest tightened at the thought of being sent away again to a strange place with unfamiliar people.

Grandmother turned to her, hazel eyes moist. "Believe me, that's the last thing I want."

"No." Sarah shook her head. "This is our home. Our baby should be born here."

～

Despite the morning's snowy surprise, a dour mood descended upon Sarah with the suggestion that she might need to leave the city. Thankfully, Jacob could stay with her on this longest night of the year.

She sat cross-legged on the bed as he rubbed her shoulders. "Do you think Grandmother's right that I might have to leave here?"

"No." He pressed his thumb on a stubborn knot. "I think she loves you and she's scared, so she's being overprotective."

The notion of her stoic and steadfast grandmother being scared was a little frightening in and of itself.

"Besides, wherever you and the baby are, I will be," he whispered in her ear. "And I can't just up and leave the city."

Sarah rolled her shoulders back, her tired muscles relaxing at her husband's comforting words and touch. "How will we raise him? The Heir to the Sacred Fire? And how different from other children do you think he'll be?" All the questions that ran through her mind lately came tumbling out on this quiet winter night.

"I think we'll do the best we can, with lots of prayer." He slid his hand down Sarah's arm to her rounded belly. "The baby moved! I just felt him move."

"Yes, just a little flutter." She placed her hand on Jacob's.

"That's amazing. When did it start?"

"Yesterday." With a yawn, she lay down on the bed. "I wish I knew more about babies. There were a few times at the orphanage when Seth brought a rescued mother and baby. I helped Elena take care of them until they were strong enough to move on." As to where, she never heard.

Jacob stretched out on his side next to her. "Then you know a lot more than I do."

She turned to him. "But will it be enough?"

"I know that our son will be very blessed to have you as his mother." He propped his head on his elbow. "Now we have an important matter to attend to."

"What's that?"

His lips formed a smile. "We need to decide on a name for him."

17

UNWORTHY

Hannah would have welcomed a cup of tea to calm her nerves, but no such hospitality was forthcoming from the high priest on this visit. Instead, he paced back and forth across his study.

"After badgering me months ago to let Jacob and Sarah get on with their life together, you now insist on continued secrecy. I threatened to send them to a distant village, and you begged me not to." He paused to warm his hands by the hearth. "Now you say their marriage and Sarah's pregnancy must stay hidden because the holy city isn't safe for her. That dark spirits are threatening their baby, and a previously unknown group of fortunetellers is proclaiming Arxmeus will rise again. This is utter madness."

"Matthias, how many signs and portents do you need to see that the end of the age is upon us? The versarius after Sarah, Jacob's healing power, his vision of the Heir, the snow at the Awakening, Ezra's prophecy."

"Do you realize what you're asking?" He raked his fingers through his graying hair. "The Fourth Scroll? The last of the

Sacred Scrolls that has been sealed for over two thousand years."

"I don't make this request of you lightly. And what of your prophecy of Sarah as a peacemaker, which has come to pass in an unexpected way?"

The high priest shook his head. "Any prophecy of mine doesn't mean much."

"Why would you say such a thing?" Hannah asked, her brow crinkled with confusion. Then again, he'd never experienced the peace that Sarah could call forth, though he certainly could do with some at the moment.

He returned to his high-backed chair and crossed his arms over his chest as if to hold himself in place. "What if you're wrong?"

"What if we're right? Who better to be the parents of the Heir to the Sacred Fire than a peacemaker and a healer? What if the Fourth Scroll contains vital instructions that we need now?"

"I've been through this with Jacob. I just don't have enough to go on to risk such a drastic step."

"Then seek the answers in prayer. Ask for a fresh vision in the Sacred Fire."

He stroked his beard. "You make it sound so easy."

"Maybe not easy, but you are the high priest of Aclesia, the leader of all the faithful."

"I have sought many a vision to no avail. I have beseeched the living God on my knees for answers." His gaze fell to the dying fire in the grate. "But the years, they pass in silence. The visions no longer come."

She leaned forward. "Surely they will come again."

"I am not that zealous young man anymore, Hannah." He sighed. "I'm just an old caretaker priest overseeing the dashed hopes of my once glorious house."

"Aren't all the Sons of Eleazar caretakers? For this very end...the coming of the Heir to the Sacred Fire and the age of peace."

He gave a stilted laugh. "We should be so fortunate to have the age of peace come in our lifetime. But no, when my end comes, I too will turn to dust in the crypts below, like all the high priests before me."

A shudder passed through her at the sight of the black-robed High Priest Matthias stricken with doubt and despair.

"And what will be the state of the House of Eleazar when Peter's time comes?" He waved a hand morosely. "He's a gifted orator, but as a priest and scholar, he leaves much to be desired."

"He's got time yet to mature. Maybe marriage and fatherhood will bring greater appreciation for his responsibilities to the faithful, as well as his family."

He shook his head. "Peter can barely read the forgotten language or write a coherent sermon. He's lost without Jacob's knowledge and steady counsel. Together, the priesthood just might survive another generation."

"If you want the House of Eleazar to survive for the coming Heir, we need to know what to do, and I believe soon. The longer we wait, the harder this gets."

He slapped his palm on his desk. "Yes, and the messier it will be explaining that Jacob got married behind my back and fathered a child, and we kept it a secret." He took a deep breath. "But that pales in comparison to the Fourth Scroll. If I open it by mistake, it will be my eternal shame, in addition to my long list of earthly failures."

"I know you've carried a heavy burden over the long and lonely years, my friend." Hannah sighed, torn between compassion and frustration. "But at such a time as this, we need your help, your leadership."

He jabbed a finger at her. "Here's what I do know. This sacred task can't possibly fall to me...because I am not worthy of it."

"But Matthias, perhaps we're not called to be worthy, only obedient."

18

CALLING INTERRUPTED

Sandwiched between her grandmother and Marta, Sarah caught a glimpse of her future sister-in-law seated with her parents on the front row. Sapphires adorned Cecilia's ears, and a thin golden band perched on her head, holding her long black tresses in place. The sparkling blue gems perfectly matched her mother's high-necked dress and the trim on her father's cloak.

"Can you see her?" Marta whispered, too short to catch a glimpse over the sea of bobbing heads.

"Yes, but she just keeps staring straight ahead, so I can't get a good look at her face."

Could Cecilia feel all the eyes on her? This stunningly beautiful young lady who had won the heart of Peter, or at least the approval of his father. Other girls and young women stared at the back of her perfectly coiffed head with a mix of anger and awe.

The arrival of Peter's fiancée was the talk of the holy city in recent days. The handsome couple was to be the star attraction at a dinner reception that evening in the Great Hall. Jacob would attend without Sarah, of course. When the festivities were over, Matthias would break the scandalous news to the Bethulians that Jacob had gone behind his back and married beneath them all.

High notes sounded, and the boys' choir led the jubilant processional into the nave, as if celebrating a wedding instead of the sacred calling of all the faithful. The students and teachers ascended the short flight of stairs to the chancel, casting subtle glances at Cecilia before taking their seats at the end of their chant.

The door in the north transept opened, and the high priest entered with Peter and Jacob close behind. As their father climbed the stairs to his ornate pulpit, Peter strode across the front of the nave and sat next to his future bride, who gave him a slight nod in her regal manner. Jacob sat alone on the front row on Sarah's side of the nave.

Would she one day sit with Jacob when the high priest's resentment and the need for secrecy ended? If it ended. Plenty of other young ladies in attendance would be happy to sit with Jacob, especially now that they knew Peter was taken.

"Hearken unto me, all ye faithful." The high priest looked out over the nave, then directed his gaze to Cecilia and her family. "And greetings to our Bethulian guests. You honor us with your presence, and we pray your time with us will be a blessing."

As he unrolled an aged scroll, Sarah tried to remember another instance when the high priest had acknowledged specific visitors. He began to read from the Second Scroll of the ancient covenant between Patrimus and Eleazar and the calling of the priesthood.

When his father concluded, Peter rose to light the prayer incense. As he prayed in the forgotten language, Sarah added her own silent prayer for acceptance and reconciliation, a lasting peace in her new family, the House of Eleazar.

Peter returned to Cecilia and bent close to whisper to her. Her perfect posture never changed.

Jacob rose with his black, leatherbound book. Then he read of the days after Kadmiel's defeat, of the return of the faithful remnant after their long years of persecution and captivity, of hiding in the mountains and fighting for survival. Together, they gathered on the High Plain of Nirel, drawn by the mysterious fire that burned from Uriel's staff, a beacon in the night calling them home.

A shiver raced up Sarah's spine. Because of the baby in her womb, would she have to spend her days hiding from those who sought to avenge their dark Lord Kadmiel by destroying her and her child?

On the front row, Cecilia stifled a yawn with her gloved hand.

The holy narrative took a turn for the better with the planting of the fields surrounding Havilah that provided grain for the Bread of Life thousands of years later. With a touch of familial pride, Sarah smiled at her grandmother, matriarch of the House of Magdala, and steward of those same blessed fields.

One of the bronze doors at the back of the nave opened, prompting whispers and looks of disapproval at the late arrivals.

"From this day forth, the foothills of the holy mountain shall be the possession of the faithful remnant." Jacob raised his voice a notch to talk over the disturbance. "In your hands, the provisions of Patrimus will be assured. So break up this fallow ground, and plant a new harvest that all may eat of the Bread of Life. But take heed, you must also sow the seeds of justice, mercy, and kindness so that this harvest will be greater than any that has come before."

At the sound of fearful gasps, Sarah turned in her seat.

"And so with each new generation, the faithful grew in

number, and the earth yielded its increase." Jacob narrowed his eyes as a small group of unkempt men entered the nave.

"We want to see the healer," one of the men shouted.

A slender priest stepped into the aisle to block their way. "This is entirely inappropriate. I must ask you to leave." His low voice carried in the confused silence.

A bearded man in a coarse canvas jacket shoved the protesting Brother aside. Behind him, two men carried a man under his shoulders, his thin legs trailing behind, limp feet dragging on the stone floor.

Matthias stood to face them. "What is the meaning of this?"

One of the men pointed at Jacob. "Please, my brother has been lame since he was a child. We know you can help him."

His stained pants in tatters, the man's gaunt face was downcast, as if he despised not just his condition, but being the object of attention and pity.

The high priest straightened his ceremonial purple vestment. "I see."

Several women near the aisle placed their handkerchiefs over their noses and mouths as if accosted by an unwelcome smell. Cecilia turned, her kohl-lined eyes widening in revulsion at the paralyzed man and his grubby friends in such close proximity. Peter rose to stand in front of her as she recoiled into her father's broad shoulder.

Another clamor began near the back. The slender priest slid out of the way as five soldiers rushed into the nave. Swords drawn, they clanked toward the motley group.

"Put away your weapons," Matthias commanded. "You have no authority here."

A soldier with an insignia of a flame on his chest sheathed his blade. "I beg to differ, Father. These men were spotted sneaking over the wall. They have no papers or right to be in the Heights."

"They do have a right to be here according to the original

agreement that the council reneged on over a decade ago," Matthias countered. "As a matter of law, the gate must be open to all who wish to enter on the holy days."

"They didn't come through the gate, and my orders are to arrest any trespassers and deliver them to the magistrate."

"We've tried the gate, but we always get turned away," one of the bedraggled men protested.

"Perhaps because you didn't have papers then either," the officer said, his voice even.

But the low vibration behind Sarah's eyes warned that anger was rising on both sides.

"I understand your concern." Matthias addressed the soldier. "But you needn't bother with these men since we've already established they are not trespassing."

"In the eyes of my commander, they are."

Matthias turned to Jacob, who had moved closer to the suffering man. "While the officer and I resolve this situation, why don't you give our guest a piece of bread and the blessing of restored health."

The guards looked to their superior who motioned for them to hold their positions.

Sarah massaged her temple as Jacob turned toward the trays of bread behind the lectern. Caleb, who normally brought the bread forward, appeared frozen in place. Peter walked over and took a heaping tray of bread made by Sarah and Marta's own hands, and brought it to Jacob.

"In the name of the living God..." He laid his hand on the man's bony shoulder. "May the Bread of Life strengthen and heal you to walk a new path from this day forward."

Sarah gripped Marta's arm as Jacob placed a piece of bread between the man's grasping fingers. His hand shaking, he brought the morsel to his mouth, the task made more difficult by his brothers holding him under the armpits.

"There, he got his blessing." The ranking soldier placed his hand on the hilt of his sword. "Now they're coming with us."

"No, they're not," Matthias countered as several soldiers surrounded the ragtag group of men. "You have no basis to bring charges against them."

One of the paralyzed man's brothers jabbed a finger at the officer. "Yeah, you can't arrest us."

Peter sprang to his father's side as the cluster of men continued to argue matters of law and order. Like a prop in the unfolding drama, the paralyzed man was pulled in varying directions as his brothers waved their arms at the soldiers to emphasize their point.

Sarah tensed on the hard pew, close enough to feel the effects of the conflict but too distant to reach any of them with her touch. Lest there be bloodshed, a three-word prayer to summon a power much greater than hers hung on her lips.

Her eyes sought her husband's, but he just stared at the broken man before him who, ever so slowly, pulled one crooked foot forward.

Low murmurs swept through the nave. When the man dragged his other foot beneath him, the heated argument faded into stunned silence. Several women dabbed at their eyes with their handkerchiefs.

"Let go of me," the man said in a hoarse voice. "Set me on my feet."

With tears in their eyes, the man's friends released him. He swayed for a moment on spindly legs, but he found his balance. Then he lifted his face to the towering stained glass of Uriel holding his flaming staff high, the gift of golden grain piled at his feet.

Sarah heard a few sniffles in her vicinity as a soldier held out his hand to Jacob. "Can I have a piece of that too?"

While her husband doled out bread and blessings, her

father-in-law turned to face them, his arms spread wide. "Brothers and sisters in the faith, heed your calling. Come and partake of the Bread of Life."

SARAH's back ached as she arranged another tray of cheeses, dried fruits, and pickled vegetables for the open house her grandmother hosted after the Calling every year. Her apron hung loosely to conceal her condition in case any guests wandered back to the kitchen by mistake. George reported the parlor and dining room were abuzz with conversation about Jacob healing the paralyzed man.

"Thank goodness, people are finally leaving." Marta returned to the kitchen with several empty platters. "You'd better make a start on the dishes. Otherwise, we'll be up till midnight."

"I won't make it to nine o'clock," Sarah said as Marta hurried away with a new tray of delicacies.

Five minutes later, the trays were soaking in warm soapy water. As she reached for a clean dish cloth, an arm snaked around her waist from behind.

She stifled a scream. "What are you doing here?"

"I missed you," Jacob said in a low voice. "But it looks like you're having fun without me."

"I'm stuck in the kitchen doing dishes because I'm pregnant, and it appears I have no husband."

"But you do." He nuzzled Sarah's neck. "One who loves you very much."

She turned and swatted him with a dish cloth. "Then help me with these dishes."

"All right. What do you need me to do?"

"I'll wash and you dry."

"So where do I stand?"

Sarah pointed to her right. "Don't you know how to do dishes?"

"I never had kitchen duty as a student."

Sarah flung a handful of soap suds at him. "I guess being the son of the high priest has its perks."

Laughing, he pulled her into a soapy embrace. "That was one of the few."

"What's going on back here?" Her grandmother strode into the kitchen.

Sarah tucked a wet strand of hair behind her ear. "Jacob's trying to help me with the dishes but failing miserably."

"You two need to keep the noise down." She wagged a bony finger at them. "If anyone realizes Jacob's here, there'll be a stampede to the kitchen."

"Wait, aren't you supposed to be at a banquet for Peter and Cecilia?" Sarah asked him.

He groaned. "It starts soon, but I don't think I can take any more of her today."

"What happened?" Grandmother asked.

"Cecilia pouted all afternoon about not being the center of attention at the Calling. Half an hour ago, she actually burst into tears complaining to Peter about how their big day was ruined."

"That's awful." Sarah liked her future sister-in-law less all the time. Not even Peter deserved such a self-centered bride.

"Apparently, she would have preferred I not healed that man and the whole lot had been hauled off to the jailor."

Grandmother shook her head in disgust. "How much longer will they be here?"

"Several more days."

"After they leave, we need to come up with a plan to get Sarah out of the city if the situation becomes too dangerous."

"What? No." Sarah exclaimed. Hiding in the holy city was bad enough, but leaving it would be even worse.

"Dear, it's becoming harder to keep your pregnancy hidden," Grandmother said.

"I know that." At almost seven months pregnant, there was no more chalking up her rounded abdomen to consuming too much bread.

"Look, I have to be with Sarah when the baby's born," Jacob said. "And I can't just leave the city."

"Besides, I haven't sensed anything unusual lately," Sarah added. "When it comes to dark spirits, things seem quiet."

"That doesn't mean our enemies aren't at work," Grandmother replied. "Surely they're searching for you."

Jacob rubbed his chin. "Maybe Peter and I took care of the problem at the fortuneteller's a few months back."

"I'd very much like to believe that." Grandmother's hazel eyes seemed pained. "But we still have no idea who the Seer is, or even if it's a man or a woman. For the last couple of months, we've hit nothing but dead ends."

Jacob pushed his dark wavy hair off his face. "Maybe there is no Seer, and that demon lied just to confuse us."

"Perhaps...but are we not in agreement there's something strange about the growing number of fortunetellers and diviners in the holy city?"

"But Sarah and I should be the ones making the decisions." Jacob's volume rose with his anger and panic.

With a reluctant nod, Grandmother ceded the point. "But we need a contingency plan, at least."

Sarah reached for his hand. "It won't hurt to have a plan, and we'll all pray we never have to use it."

"If it comes to it, Sarah and I can live together at the cathedral. She and the baby would be safe there."

"And your father will go along with that?"

His gaze dropped to the floor. "I'd convince him. Besides,

the House of Eleazar's survived many threats over the centuries. Why would we run now?"

"Because we're not just nearing the end of Sarah's pregnancy. We're nearing the end of the age." Grandmother squeezed the silver band on her finger. "And the stakes grow ever higher."

19

CONSPIRACY THEORY

Hannah's fellow council members nodded in greeting as she entered the third-floor chamber of the Hall of Justice. Banners of the First Families lined the walls on either side of a long marble table. At the far end of the vaulted room, a fire blazed in the wide stone fireplace. Commander Xavier, head of the city guard, conferred with a few other men in hushed tones near a window overlooking the gardens.

Hannah took her seat at the table next to the kindly octogenarian, Councilor Jedidiah. A cough racked his withered body as he attempted to welcome her. While she feared he wasn't long for this world, the Arcanus clan looked forward to his passing, after which, they'd install one of their allies in his position to further tip the council in their favor.

Matthias sat across from her looking like he'd rather be anywhere else. Sebastian, the treasurer of the council, slumped in the chair next to him, staring vacantly at his reports. Weighed down by grief, the man seemed to have aged at least five years since losing his daughter to the versarius last winter.

A shudder coursed through Hannah. She could have lost

Sarah as well had Jacob and Peter not put an end to that demonic monstrosity. At least Sebastian had his son, seated behind him, to lead their house into the future.

The rest of the councilors hastened to their seats as a rhythmic tapping in the hallway grew louder. Sylvaneus Arcanus paused in the doorway, one manicured hand resting on his gold inlaid cane. When he reached the head of the table, he smoothed his silver hair, then handed his assistant his cloak and cane. The pretentious prop couldn't support his ample weight but could be used for swatting any unfortunate person in his path. The harried assistant retreated to one of the wooden benches against the wall, where advisors, family members, and hired help listened to the proceedings.

Hannah's jaw clenched as she glanced over her shoulder at the green and gold crest of the House of Magdala on the wall behind her. She could never invite her rightful heirs, Sarah and Jonah, lest the silver haired snake at the head of the table discover they were alive.

Or his son, Niccolus Arcanus, who just sauntered into the meeting wearing the flowing black robe of the chief magistrate, as if anyone needed to be reminded of his position. He wore his straight dark hair slicked back like his father, but his slimmer build and sharp features came from his late mother.

He swept past his father on the way to his chair, slowing only to admire the ample bosom of Councilor Cornelius's much younger wife. As he passed, his pant leg brushed her shapely calf. Niccolus was rumored to keep a mistress or two, but a blatant advance on a councilman's wife ten feet behind his back was low, even by Arcanus standards.

Sylvaneus cleared his throat, his triple chins wobbling like jelly. "Our primary order of business today is to discuss the grave ramifications of what transpired at the Calling ceremony last week."

Hannah pursed her lips. Only an Arcanus would view the

miracle of a lame man walking again as a matter of deep concern.

Sylvaneus narrowed his eyes at the high priest. "And the security situation arising from the alleged healing that took place."

"What was that?" Jedidiah cupped his hand over his ear. "Healing?"

Sylvaneus barely spared the old man a glance as another coughing fit ensued. "Some have suggested you're perpetuating a fraud."

"Who are the 'some' you reference?" Matthias folded his hands on the table. "Were they among the thousand in attendance at the Calling?"

"That I wouldn't know." Sylvaneus waved his hand. "But rumors are spreading that your son Jacob is the prophesied Heir to the Sacred Fire. Or some such nonsense."

"We've never made such a claim," Matthias said. "Nor would we."

"Good, then see to it that you dispel this foolish notion right away, before it incites the populace further."

"Incites them to what?" Matthias's dark eyes found Hannah's for a fleeting moment. "Hope in the fulfillment of divine prophecy?"

Did that mean he was coming around to the idea of his future grandson being the Heir?

Sylvaneus's nostrils flared. "Incites them to false hope...or whatever it is you're peddling these days."

"I personally witnessed this healing," Councilor Miranda cut in. "I can assure you it was a sight to behold."

Hannah barely suppressed a smile at the petite woman coming to the high priest's aid.

"I too was there at the Calling," said another. "It was quite miraculous."

"Father Matthias, isn't that the same fellow who lay begging outside the north gate for years?" Hannah asked, despite knowing the answer.

"Yes, the poor man had been lame since childhood."

"Then the suggestion that he laid in the mud for decades pretending to be paralyzed only to spring some hoax now is absurd," Hannah said.

"Yes. Can we not rejoice that this man is healed and move on to other business?" asked Miranda, her patience seeming to wear thin.

Sylvaneus bristled. "This is a serious breach. It creates all sorts of security complications for the holy city, especially the Heights."

"People want the gate open for your son's healing service." Niccolus sneered at Matthias. "Who knows what other dregs will be headed our way when news of this spreads through the countryside? And it must have been embarrassing with the esteemed Bethulians there to celebrate their daughter's betrothal to your eldest son."

"I don't believe our guests were ever in any danger," Matthias countered.

Commander Xavier leaned forward, his uniform straining against his bulging biceps. "Are you an expert in security matters now?"

"Hardly." Matthias squared his shoulders. "But if you're concerned about this so-called breach of security, I should think you'd take that up with your soldiers."

Councilor Miranda sniffed. "Yes, if they were so unobservant that a band of men scaled the wall fifty feet from their post, how can any of us have confidence in our safety?"

Sebastian looked up from his stack of papers. "How indeed?"

Matthias held up his hand. "Councilors, I believe I can allay some of your concerns. My son Jacob will conduct two additional healing services per week...outside the Heights."

Miranda looked down her pointed nose. "That would seem to be a reasonable solution."

Others nodded around the table.

"But this cannot stand." Niccolus slapped his palm on the table. "Commander Xavier, we must make an example of this filth by bringing charges against them."

"I think that would prove a deeply unpopular decision." Hannah turned to him. "That poor man had been imprisoned in his broken body since childhood, and now that he's been made well, you would jail him and his friends?"

"Niccolus, you of all people should know that's legally dubious," Sebastian added.

"And what good would it accomplish?" asked another councilor as the elder Arcanus silently fumed at the head of the table.

"The purpose of this council should be to reduce tensions in the city." Hannah trained her gaze on Niccolus. "Another unjust sentence would only create more resentment and add fuel to the fire."

20

———

LATE TO THE PARTY

Sarah opened the front door. "Jonah, you didn't have to get me anything."

"According to our grandmother, I did." He stepped into the hallway and handed her a drooping bouquet of daffodils.

"They're beautiful. Thank you."

"Happy birthday." He bent and kissed her cheek.

Marta appeared in the front hallway. "I'll find a vase for those while you two join the others in the parlor."

Jonah eyed the festive dining room table set for eight. "I'm starving. When do we eat?"

"We're still waiting for Jacob." Sarah passed Marta her flowers.

"So? That's his problem he's late."

Marta gave him the side-eye. "Punctuality isn't exactly your strong suit either."

Sarah led her brother into the parlor where Thaniel and Cornelia were admiring the old rocking chair and bassinet Grandmother had refinished for her as a birthday gift. A forest green baby blanket from Marta and George lay inside the bassinet, along with a collection of baby clothes sewn by Cornelia.

"I can still picture your sweet mother rocking you in this chair." Cornelia's eyes glistened.

"And me too?" Jonah asked.

Grandmother chuckled. "I can still picture your mother trying desperately to get you to stop howling from your colic."

"Oh, thanks for that." He crossed his arms over his chest.

"So, does the new little one have a name yet?" Cornelia asked.

"Yes." Sarah placed her hand on her belly to feel a tiny kick.

"And?" Cornelia peered at her excitedly.

"Apparently it's tradition in the House of Eleazar not to divulge the baby's name until after it's born."

Cornelia's face fell.

"Marta is just as disappointed, but I'm afraid you'll all have to wait a little longer."

Jacob arrived about five minutes later, and Marta hustled everyone into the dining room before her roast dried out.

"Sorry I'm late." He pulled a chair out for Sarah. "I got summoned to pray for Councilor Jedidiah, who was practically on his death bed."

"Poor Jedidiah has been ailing for months. He looked dreadful at our last council meeting." Grandmother took her seat at the mahogany table.

"Well, he should be up and around tomorrow," Jacob said.

"Oh, my." She chuckled. "It'll be hard for some members of the council to accuse you and your father of fraud when you healed one of our own members. Not that Sylvaneus and his cronies won't try."

Seated next to Sarah, Jonah listened intently as Jacob recounted healing the councilman, and others earlier in the day at a market outside the Heights.

Jonah turned to her. "I always thought you were just weird,

but there's something about the way you can calm people and bring peace to a situation."

"Thanks, I guess."

"And Jacob heals sick people—even a fellow who couldn't walk." He reached for his water goblet. "I don't know much about prophecy and old scrolls and stuff, but I want to be anointed too."

Thaniel stroked his goatee, suppressing a grin. "Prophecies and old scrolls can be truly fascinating."

Sarah's eyes found her grandmother's. They'd decided not to tell Jonah yet about her baby being the prophesied Heir to the Sacred Fire. Learning their full family history was enough for the time being, and he wasn't always disciplined about what came out of his teenage mouth.

"Being anointed with the Sacred Fire is not a matter to be taken lightly," Grandmother said. "But if you want to be anointed, you may come back next month for the ceremony."

"Of course, you can stay with us again," Thaniel said.

"Yes, you always liven things up," Cornelia added.

Sarah smiled across the table at the generous couple who would host Jonah in their home tonight as well. Because of his strong resemblance to their late father, Grandmother didn't want him spending too much time at the bakery. Hopefully, anyone who might be paying attention would assume he was a distant relative of Thaniel and Cornelia's, not the cursed son of Thaddeus Asher.

"That's a nice present for your sister on her birthday," Marta said to him. "Better than wilted flowers anyway."

George pointed at Jonah's empty plate. "And you do love a good feast."

He helped himself to the last piece of pot roast. "Definitely an added benefit."

Sarah passed him the bread basket too. "But I seem to recall last year you were worried Jacob would set your hair on fire. Then you ran from the square."

"No, I didn't..." His cheeks colored. "You must be thinking of someone else."

"I've yet to set anyone's hair on fire." Jacob shrugged. "Then again, there's a first time for everything."

She laughed. "I would recommend you stay away from Peter though."

"Yes, don't go anywhere near my brother. He's not a fan of yours." Jacob draped his arm over Sarah's shoulder. "I also have a present for you, and I think I can top wilted flowers." He reached into his coat pocket and removed a silver chain with a glass pendant in the shape of a teardrop.

"That's all you got the mother of your child...a trinket." Jonah smirked. "I figured you were cheap."

"It's beautiful." Sarah tilted her head. "Look how it catches the light. It seems like it has a tiny flame inside."

"Want me to put it on you?" Jacob asked.

"Please." Sarah swept her hair off her neck so he could fasten the clasp.

Marta blinked in amazement. "Goodness, I could swear there's a fire inside."

"It certainly looks that way." Cornelia leaned closer. "How pretty."

"I can even see it reflected in your eyes, my dear," Thaniel said.

"Grandmother, hold still for a moment." Sarah held up her pendant. The reflection of a tiny dancing flame shone in her dark pupils. "I can see it in your eyes too."

Jonah's brow furrowed. "I don't know what you people are talking about. It looks like a misshapen piece of glass in tarnished silver to me."

"You can't see the fire inside?" But then Sarah couldn't see it in his eyes either.

"What fire?" Jonah threw up his hands. "How much wine have you people had?"

George laughed. "Maybe you need spectacles."

He huffed. "I see just fine."

Jacob waved a hand at Jonah. "You're the only one here who's never been anointed. Maybe that has something to do with it."

Jonah looked around the table. "All of you can see a flame in there?"

"Yes, very clearly." Sarah nodded with the others.

"Huh, I really better get some of that fire too."

"How intriguing." Grandmother stared at Sarah's pendant. "But whatever the case, this necklace must be the work of a highly skilled craftsman."

"Yeah, I bet that set you back," George said.

Jacob shifted on his chair. "No, it really didn't."

"Wherever did you find such an unusual piece?" Thaniel asked.

"Uh...at the cathedral."

Sarah looked up at him, and his mouth quirked into that mischievous smile she loved so much.

"I wanted something extra special for you on your first birthday as my wife. I noticed this hidden away in an old cabinet, and it just seemed meant for you."

An old cabinet? Hidden away? Her hand reached for the mysterious pendant that lay close to her heart. From the underground scroll room perhaps?

"You found it?" Jonah rolled his eyes. "See, you really are cheap."

21

THE BURNING ONE

Jacob pushed the last of his pickled beets around his plate. His father had insisted he dine in the Great Hall tonight with the other teaching priests and students. If they intended to keep Sarah's pregnancy secret for a while longer, he would have to stick to a normal routine. He set down his fork and looked out over the long tables of chattering boys. Not only did he much prefer his wife's company but also Marta's cooking.

As his father stood, a hush spread from their head table to the banner of the white flame at the far end of the great hall. Then his father dismissed the restless students to enjoy their hour of free time before evening prayers. Jacob would use this opportunity to pay a brief visit to the bakery.

But before he could join the rush of boys leaving, his father turned to him, brow creased. "I believe we're missing something important."

"Missing something?" Jacob froze. "What do you mean?"

"I'd forgotten about it for years, but it might be relevant now."

"What is it?" He prayed it wasn't a teardrop necklace his

father suddenly remembered. Could his father have paid a visit to the Scroll Room in the last couple days and discovered it gone?

"Get your brother." His father gestured to the huge stone hearth where Peter stood talking with several older students. "We're going to the library."

"The library..." Jacob exhaled. At least nothing could land him in trouble there.

He retrieved Peter, who was being congratulated on his engagement to Cecilia, arguably one of the most beautiful women in all of Aclesia. Since her visit and the announcement of their betrothal, Peter held his head higher. Jacob suspected as soon as he and Cecilia were married, he'd get busy trying to produce a son of his own. Meanwhile, Jacob was alone in his efforts to convince their father to open the Fourth Scroll.

A few minutes later, the three of them reached the library, although their father had yet to divulge the purpose of their visit. Several boys huddled around an oil lamp with their open books. Their eyes widened at the entrance of the high priest.

"It would be best if we had privacy," their father said in a low voice.

"Out you go, boys." Peter waved them toward the door. "You know, you really should find something more interesting to do with your time," he added as they hustled past.

Jacob expected his father to unlock the door to the restricted collection, but instead, he made his way slowly down a row of shelves devoted to prophecies and related commentaries. He selected an old scroll, then unrolled it on the table the boys had abandoned.

"What is this, Father?" Jacob moved the oil lamp closer.

His father pointed to a passage halfway down the parchment. "A miscellaneous little prophecy written by High Priest Malachi that isn't included in any of his bound books."

"Out of the north comes one who will bring peace," Jacob

translated from the forgotten language. "After an appointed time, a spirit of truth shall blow across the land. Eyes will be opened, and ears will hear anew of the might of the living God and his unquenchable fire."

"Nice and succinct," Peter said. "If that's all, can I go now?"

With a slight shake of his head, their father continued. "When I was a student, I wrote an essay on this passage arguing the common interpretation was lacking, that it wasn't about Brother Joshua at all. But my teacher said I didn't demonstrate sufficient support for my thesis and gave me a failing grade on the assignment." He scowled. "I'm still angry about it."

Peter shrugged. "I never had a problem getting over that sort of thing."

"Probably because you deserved all your bad marks." Jacob pointed to the date over two hundred years ago. "This was written just before the siege on the holy city."

"War was imminent." Father nodded. "But I always thought it a stretch to say that Joshua brought peace, even though he did come from the north."

Jacob pictured the statue of Joshua, the warrior priest, brandishing his sword near the stairway to the crypts. "Yeah, that doesn't seem to make sense."

"Although he brought vital information that ultimately led to Cedrian's defeat," his father added.

Jacob lifted his head as bells rang faintly at the front door to the school.

"Caleb will see to it." His father smoothed the dry parchment. "Note the use of the gender-neutral subject in 'comes one who will bring peace.'"

Jacob's eyebrows shot up. "It could be either a man or woman."

"Ah, maybe a woman we all know." Peter said. "Now can I leave?"

"Out of the north comes one who will bring peace," Jacob

repeated softly. If Father believed this pertained to Sarah, would he finally agree to open the Fourth Scroll?

"And crucially, neither High Priest Malachi nor his daughter Deborah wrote anything to indicate the fulfillment of that prophecy in their lifetimes," his father added.

Jacob leaned over the table. "Could it partially be about Joshua but also point to a future event like the end of the age?" He held his breath, awaiting his father's response to his loaded question.

"That's certainly possible." He nodded.

Caleb appeared in the doorway. "Father Matthias, a lady's here to see you. She says it's urgent." He twisted his hands. "She seems upset, crying. Can you come, please?"

Peter moved toward the door. "How about I go see what the poor woman needs since I'm no use here?"

"Have her wait in your study, and I'll be along shortly. And Caleb, ask the kitchen to prepare tea."

"What do you think the rest of it means...a spirit of truth?" Jacob turned back to the scroll. "That part fits in the sense that eyes were opened to Cedrian's evil."

His father stroked his beard. "There was a reawakening of faith under Joshua's leadership as the chief priest of Taberah, but—"

An anguished scream rang out.

Jacob sprinted into the main corridor, but it was empty.

Another shriek sounded nearby.

"This way!" His father pulled him toward the front hallway.

Jacob flew past him and skidded around the corner.

A plume of acrid gray smoke rose in the hall outside his brother's study. Beneath it, Peter writhed on the floor, his hands clawing at his face.

"Peter!" Jacob crouched next to him, a sharp smell like vinegar and burning flesh stinging his nostrils. "What happened?"

Their father knelt beside Peter. "He must have been taken by surprise."

"Father, your robe!" Green-gray vapor swirled around his knee on the floor.

His father leapt to his feet, the toxin burning a hole in the black wool. He slipped out of his long robe, and it fell in a smoldering heap.

"We've got to get this poison off him." Jacob raced into his study and grabbed the carafe of water behind his desk.

His father moved back a few steps while he poured the water over Peter's head. He twitched as the water ran off his reddened skin, then with a moan reached for his face again.

A metallic crash sounded down the hall behind them.

His mouth hanging open, Caleb gripped an empty tray, a teapot rolling at his feet.

"Bring holy water from the cistern," Jacob called to him. "As much as you can carry. Hurry!"

"Get Brother Augustus and the others," Father shouted as Caleb sprinted away.

Jacob leaned over Peter. "Try to keep his hands away from his face so I can get a better look."

His father strained to hold Peter's forearms while Jacob inspected the angry blisters rising on the reddened skin around his eyes, which were squeezed shut.

Brother Augustus lumbered toward them with several other teachers close behind. "Father Matthias, what's happened?"

"Peter's been attacked."

Students crowded into the end of the corridor, their curiosity turning to horror at the sight of the black robed figure on the floor.

"Get all the students to their rooms now," Father thundered. "The attacker may still be in the cathedral."

"Yes, Father."

Jacob prayed silently for healing while his father barked

orders to secure the dormitories, his study, and the back hallway.

The hallway to the Scroll Room? Jacob's eyes flitted to his father's grim face as he turned back toward Peter. Would the attacker know to search for the Fourth Scroll? Could she possibly find it?

"Summon the city guard," he added over his shoulder. "And Augustus, we believe the attacker is a woman."

"A woman?" repeated Augustus as gasps echoed behind him.

Just then, Caleb rounded the corner with a sloshing jar of holy water.

Jacob took the heavy jar from his panting cousin and doused Peter's head, hands, and chest. With a hiss, a tremendous cloud of white steam arose. Then his brother went limp on the cold stone.

SARAH SET the book she was reading on the end table and massaged her temples. The mild headache she'd had all evening was only getting worse. Marta had already retired for the evening, and George was finishing the kitchen prep for the next day's work. Maybe the best thing for her headache would be to go to bed soon too.

Her grandmother entered the parlor bearing two steaming cups of tea, given her staunch belief that tea could help cure all ills. "I added some extra honey for you."

"Do you hear that?" Sarah inclined her head toward the front window.

Grandmother placed her tea on the small table. "What?"

"Hoof beats, but there's not usually a patrol now." Sarah rose and peaked through a narrow gap in the drapes.

"That's strange." Grandmother joined her at the window. "Sounds like the noise is coming from the Tower Gate."

"I wonder what's going on?" Sarah clutched her teardrop necklace, finding it more comforting than tea.

The lines on Grandmother's brow deepened. "I'll be certain to find out tomorrow."

Shouts went up, and a contingent of foot soldiers marched past them on the cobblestoned street.

"On second thought, I'd rather find out now." She strode to the parlor doorway and called down the hall, "George, could you come here please?"

A few moments later, his bald head poked into the room.

"What do you make of this?" Grandmother motioned to the window.

His shoulders tensed. "That's a lot of activity for this time of night. Would you like me to investigate?"

"Please, and be discreet."

He nodded. "I'll go out the back way and circle around by the Tower Gate."

"Sounds like its coming from both sides of the wall," Grandmother said after George left.

Dread rose in Sarah's chest as more shouting ensued. "Near the cathedral too."

Grandmother returned to her favorite armchair and sipped the rest of her tea, but the rapid tapping of her foot gave her worried state away.

Her head still throbbing, Sarah remained by the window, praying for peace in whatever strange events were underway.

A door slammed, and heavy footsteps sounded in the kitchen. "Back already, George?" Grandmother called into the dim hallway.

Sarah squinted out the front window again. A hulking man with his cap pulled low over his forehead hurried down the street toward the bakery. As he entered the lamplight, Sarah's breath caught at the familiar figure of George about twenty yards away. With a strangled cry, she spun around.

A black shape loomed in the parlor doorway.

Grandmother was on her feet. "Jacob, for heaven's sake."

"Sorry if I startled you." He pushed his bangs off his face.

Sarah rushed to her husband's side. "What are you doing here? Shouldn't you be at evening prayers?"

"I just needed to know you're all right," he said breathlessly.

"We're fine. What's wrong?" Sarah reached for his hand.

He pulled it away, wincing.

"What happened?" Sarah eyed the red welts on his palm.

"I'll be all right." He dropped his hand to his side. "But Peter's in far worse shape after being attacked."

"Attacked?" Sarah's hand flew to the bulge on her abdomen.

Grandmother braced herself on the arm of her chair. "How?"

"A woman came to the cathedral, apparently distraught. Caleb let her in, and Peter went to see what she needed. The next thing we knew, Peter was screaming on the floor in the hallway."

Grandmother paled. "Was he stabbed?"

"No. Whoever it was threw some sort of poison in his face."

"There's been an attack at the cathedral!" George sped into the parlor, nearly running into Jacob. "But you probably already know that."

"We just heard." Sarah cringed at the thought of Peter's ordeal.

Grandmother turned back to Jacob. "What did Peter tell you about the attacker?

"Nothing, since he's unconscious. The guards are questioning those in vicinity, but it was dark when the woman arrived at the school. They've stepped up their patrols, but we're not optimistic, especially since my father doesn't have the best relationship with them."

"And the attacker was a woman." Grandmother pursed her lips. "One of the fortunetellers?"

"Did she have frizzy red hair?" Sarah recalled the palm reader that accosted her in the market last spring.

"No. Caleb was the only one who saw her, and he said she had dark hair. But he didn't get a good look since her face was mostly covered."

"Why would someone want to hurt Peter?" Sarah asked.

"The woman asked to see Father, so it would seem he was the intended target."

"The high priest..." Grandmother drew in a sharp breath.

George ran a hand over his shiny head. "That's an odd way to attack someone though. If she wanted to kill him, there would have been better, more lethal ways."

"I'm afraid there's a certain dark logic," Jacob said. "It's not widely known outside the priesthood, but only the eyes of the high priest can look upon the Fourth Scroll."

"Of course." Grandmother turned to Sarah. "Then this situation is even more serious than I initially feared."

Sarah grimaced. Things seemed to grow more serious by the day, and in this latest battle, Peter had paid a heavy price.

George paced across the small room. "I'm sure Demetrius will send word to us tomorrow with what he learns, and I'll make some quiet inquiries too."

Grandmother frowned. "The council will most certainly use this shocking situation to tighten security and limit those who can visit the Heights."

Jacob glanced at the darkened window. "Just in time for the Anointing next week."

A shiver passed through Sarah as she recalled the palm reader's last words and hostile tone...*people of the flame.* "Maybe that's all part of the plan."

22

KEEPING VIGIL

Morning sunlight streamed through a narrow window in the south turret. Jacob stared at his brother as he lay unmoving on his bed, his sweaty hair plastered to his pillow. He and his father had taken shifts throughout the night, not that either of them got much sleep on the makeshift cot. But at least there was no evidence the attacker had attempted to locate the Scroll Room.

Jacob touched the sliver of Peter's forehead not covered by bandages. "He's still burning with fever."

"Yes, and he's been unresponsive for too long." His father rose from the chair next to the bed and rubbed his bloodshot eyes. "I sent for the physician an hour ago."

"I don't understand why I can't heal him." Jacob massaged his knotted neck. "I've cleaned his wounds and prayed over him, but nothing seems to work."

"I wish we knew more about that toxic substance, and if—"

His father broke off before he voiced a possibility Jacob didn't want to contemplate. "You think it might have been cursed?"

He let out a deep sigh. "I pray not."

Someone knocked on the sitting room door below. "The physician is here, Father Matthias," Brother Augustus called up the stairs.

"Please send him up."

Jacob met the portly man at the top of the stone staircase.

"Ah, the great healing priest I've heard so much about." The physician handed Jacob his brown cloak, which perfectly matched his bushy mustache. "Yet you can't heal your own brother?"

"His situation is perplexing." Jacob waved him toward the large four post bed. "But I certainly hope you can help him."

"I'm sure I'll have him on the mend soon."

"Thank you for coming, doctor." His father extended his hand.

"Of course, Father Matthias." He approached the sick bed. "I'm just sorry to see your son in such an unfortunate state."

"As are we."

The physician set his scuffed leather satchel on the trunk at the foot of the bed. "Could he have hit his head when he fell to the floor?"

"It's possible." Jacob stepped closer. "But I don't believe that's what's causing—"

"I will make that determination during the course of my exam." He removed a pair of spectacles from his breast pocket and perched them on his bulbous nose.

As the physician took hold of Peter's wrist, Jacob moved to the window so as not to risk another rebuke.

"What do you make of his condition, doctor?" His father asked a few minutes later. "Why doesn't he wake up?"

The physician straightened. "His lungs sound clear, pulse is rapid but otherwise regular, breathing's rather shallow. Has he been in good health, otherwise?"

"Yes, all his life."

"I'd better check the extent of his burns." He spread out a

cloth and removed Peter's bandages. Soon a soiled pile sat on the bed. "My, my, those are ugly burns."

Jacob crept closer to make his own determination but cringed at the angry pustules that pockmarked his brother's cheeks and forehead.

The physician leaned over, examining the dead skin peeling around his brother's eyes. "The handsome priest no more." He turned to Father. "You should expect significant scarring."

He removed a jar of salve from his satchel and began applying it to much of Peter's face.

After rewrapping the bandages around his head, he said, "This will help his skin heal to the greatest extent possible."

Jacob crossed his arms over his chest. Based on the fragrant smell, it seemed identical to what he had already used.

The physician straightened. "Your younger son did an adequate job of cleansing his wounds, but given this caustic substance, I'm not optimistic about the delicate eye tissue."

Father cleared his throat. "By which you mean his eyesight."

"Yes, but time will tell."

Jacob gripped the bedpost, wanting to both shake Peter out of his coma and punch their condescending visitor.

"I'm afraid there's nothing more I can do for him at the moment." The physician removed his spectacles and returned them to his coat pocket.

Jacob had his cloak ready and handed it to him.

"But when will he wake up?" his father asked.

"That, I can't say." Picking up his leather satchel, he turned toward the stairs. "There is the possibility of never."

"ARE you sure this is a good idea?" Sarah followed close behind Jacob as the flame of his torch flickered on the rough stone walls of the tunnel.

"Nobody else has been able to help him, but maybe you can." He slowed as they neared a small rounded door.

He held his finger to his lips and opened the door a crack. "All clear."

They ducked through the five-foot opening into the natural cavern beneath the cathedral. Across the underground stream, the Sacred Fire guarded the crypts, the resting place of the departed high priests.

"What if someone spots you creeping around with a very pregnant woman?" she asked as they climbed the wide stone staircase to the hall above.

"Everyone's at evening prayers right now, aside from my father who won't leave Peter's bedside."

"Your father..." Sarah slowed. "Does he know I'm coming?"

"Yes, this is definitely not the time for me to spring any more surprises on him."

Sarah didn't find his response particularly comforting. "Just how bad off is Peter?"

Jacob returned his torch to a wall sconce with a deep sigh. "I really don't know. The physician came this morning, but Peter's not getting better. At this point, Father's willing to try anything."

So bringing her to see Peter was an act of desperation on the part of the high priest.

He held a finger to his lips as they slipped into the corridor that ran under the nave. With dozens of priests and students directly above them in prayer, she moved as fast as her feet could quietly carry her.

"We're afraid he might be suffering from more than just his burns," he said in a low voice, motioning for Sarah to follow him up a half-flight of stairs to the main level. "If it were only that, he should've awoken by now."

"What does that mean?" she whispered.

His eyes scanned the empty passage. "There's the possibility that whatever poison was used on Peter could be cursed."

"Cursed?" Sarah's heart hammered as they rounded a corner. Speeding past the Great Hall, she wasn't sure which was worse...the risk of being discovered, dealing with cursed poison, or facing her father-in-law.

Near the back of the cathedral, Jacob shoved a sturdy wooden door open, and they entered the south turret, his life-long home.

Sarah glanced around the first-floor sitting room. A gray wool blanket was balled up on the leather sofa near the hearth. Dirty plates teetered on the edge of a foot stool, and trays of partially eaten food crowded a table near the stone staircase.

He cringed. "It normally doesn't look this bad."

"I would hope not."

At the base of the stairs, Jacob reached for her hand. "We don't have to stay long if you're uncomfortable."

She gave him a reassuring squeeze, and they began the climb. Near the top, Sarah peeked over the ornate banister. Matthias sat slumped in a chair next to the four-poster bed, his shirtsleeves rolled up and elbows on his knees, keeping vigil.

"Father, why don't you get some rest," Jacob said as they skirted dirty clothes and bedding piled next to a cot. "Sarah and I can stay with Peter for a while."

He turned to them, appearing more the worried parent than distinguished high priest. "Thank you for coming, Sarah."

"Of course." She clutched Jacob's hand in the presence of the man whose rejection still stung.

"I'd like to stay." Matthias's eyes traveled to her protruding belly. "But please sit."

He vacated the chair, and Sarah took his place at Peter's bedside.

"Do you think he's in pain?" she asked, trying to reconcile

the bandaged and comatose figure with her confident and energetic brother-in-law.

"Could be." Jacob leaned over the bed. "His breathing's still fast and shallow."

She reached for Peter's hand lying on top of the blanket. A small patch of skin flaked off beneath her fingertips, and she could only imagine what his face looked like under all the bandages.

Taking a deep breath to calm her racing thoughts, she probed for whatever darkness had Peter in its grip, and prayed for a divine peace to overcome it.

"*In nominees de Vivendi*," the high priest murmured from the foot of the bed, his head bent over his folded hands.

Heat reminiscent of the palm reader's harsh grip seeped into her hand, and a familiar throbbing grew behind her eyes. She drew in a sharp breath as a bitter, acidic taste formed on her tongue.

"What is it?" Jacob asked.

"I think you're right about the poison being cursed."

He ran a hand down his face. "Be very careful..."

"I know." With a baby in her womb, she did not want to try to draw this darkness out of him like she used to do for her brother.

But there might be a better way. Recalling her disturbing encounter with the palm reader, Sarah closed her eyes, and an image formed in her mind of the Sacred Fire traveling down her arm and into his prone body. Black smoke rose to meet it, a roiling oppressive darkness driven by the powerful hatred of their enemies.

Peter's mouth contorted between his bandages and a low moan escaped.

"What's happening?" Jacob laid his hand on her rigid shoulder, a hint of panic in his voice.

"He's engaged in some sort of battle within." Her eyes

closed, Sarah tightened her grip as she envisioned black tendrils coiling like a snake in the center of Peter's chest. The white fire rushed over the tumultuous poison. His body twitched as the consuming blaze destroyed the final wisps of cursed darkness.

Sarah exhaled as Peter stilled, and peace settled over them.

"Look, his breathing's back to normal," Jacob said.

"Yes, I think you're right." Matthias leaned over the bed, watching his son's chest rise and fall in a slow and steady rhythm. "Maybe now he can rest and recover." He turned to Sarah. "I don't know what you did, but thank you."

She let go of Peter's hand and massaged her temples. "I just hope it helps." This strange spiritual skirmish may have been won, but would it be enough to bring the healing and restoration needed to rouse him from his comatose state?

Jacob brought her a glass of water. "Are you well?"

She leaned back in the chair. "Just a little tired."

"You'd better get Sarah back to the tunnel before prayers end," Matthias said.

Jacob pulled out his pocket watch. "We need to hurry."

She stood, her legs shaky.

"Can you make it?" He put his arm around her waist.

"I think so." Sarah glanced at Peter resting peacefully, before moving to the staircase.

The high priest went before them on their slow trip downstairs, Sarah clinging to Jacob and the banister.

"Do you need to rest a little longer?" Matthias looked alarmed.

"No, I'll be all right." She nodded, her legs steadier now.

"Then take good care of yourself and my grandson, the next generation of the House of Eleazar."

"I will." Her eyes moistened at his acknowledgment of the baby in her womb.

She jumped as a fist banged on the sitting room door. "Father Matthias, is everything all right?"

"Yes, why?"

Jacob frantically waved her away from the door.

"I thought I heard a woman's voice," the man said.

She hurried behind the sofa and dropped to her hands and knees.

"That's probably your imagination working overtime," Matthias replied. "But just in case, please conduct another sweep of the halls and check the outer doors."

"Yes, Father."

His footsteps faded, but a few moments later the hallway filled with the voices of boys fast approaching.

"Oh, no. The prayer service just let out." Jacob helped her up, and she dusted herself off.

The high priest ran a hand over his lined forehead. "It probably would be best if you stayed the night, Sarah. And I suspect Jacob could use some peace too."

The three of them climbed the stairs again, their steps heavy with exhaustion. Matthias claimed the cot by Peter while Sarah and Jacob continued upward to his room on the third floor. She was comforted to see it was much neater than the two below.

"What if I can't heal him?" Jacob swayed on his feet.

She reached for his arm. "You need to get some rest too. Try again in the morning."

He glanced at the large four poster bed, identical to his brother's. "What if he never wakes?"

"Peter's young and strong, and we'll keep praying for him, as will many others."

"I know, but what if I can't heal anyone anymore?" He looked down at Sarah's abdomen. "What if you and the baby need me, and I can't—"

"That's not going to happen." Sarah brushed his cheek with a kiss. "We'll be all right." *Patrimus, let that be true.*

"My mother wasn't all right." His voice broke, and he turned toward the narrow window.

"No…" If only she could heal that life-long wound that cut deep in his soul. She ran her hand over her belly, grieving not just for her husband but also the woman who never had a chance to know him.

"I'm supposed to be this great healer." He scoffed. "But my brother lies in a coma, and I can't help him. What good am I?"

Sarah leaned her head against his shoulder blade and wrapped her arms around his waist. "Maybe you have helped him, and we just can't see it yet."

He shook his head. "This is not how things were supposed to be for my mother, for Peter, or for us. We should have our own home, our own life by now…not all this secrecy."

"I know, and that day will come."

"I want to believe that." A shudder ran through his chest. "But if our enemies are desperate enough to stage an attack inside the Cathedral, then no one is safe, least of all you and the baby."

23

PETER'S VISION

Sarah awoke to Jacob sitting next to her in his plush bed, his head in his hands and chest heaving. She reached over and rubbed a soothing circle on his back. "You had that nightmare again about your father."

"Yes." He turned to her, a sheen of sweat on his face. "Except it's not about my father."

"It's not? Then who?"

"Me." He sprang from the bed and reached for his pants dangling over a chair. "It's always been about me."

"What do you mean?"

He tugged on a pair of black pants. "In the dream, I'm surrounded by a swarm of people I don't recognize calling out to me, reaching for me. They're all calling 'Father Jacob, Father Jacob." He yanked on his white linen shirt. "But I can never be Father Jacob unless Peter is...dead."

"No." Sarah threw off the covers as her husband flew down the stairs to his brother's room.

She nearly ran into the back of him at the bottom of the stairs as he stood still as a statue. Steeling herself, she peered around him.

With most of his head wrapped in bandages, Peter lay propped on his bed while Matthias helped him take sips of water.

"Oh, thank heaven." She clutched Jacob's arm as he continued to stare at his brother.

"Is that Sarah here in our private quarters?" Peter felt for the covers and pulled them over his bare chest.

Jacob found his voice. "Yeah, we're both here."

"I can't believe I slept through such scandalous behavior."

"We were too worried about you for anything scandalous to occur," she said.

He coughed a couple times. "How long have I been asleep anyway?"

"About a day and a half." Matthias set the water goblet on the side table.

"That long..." Peter touched the bandages wrapped around his face.

"How do you feel?" Jacob moved to the foot of the bed.

"Well, I've been better."

"What do you remember from the attack?"

"Like I told father, she must have been hiding inside my study because I never saw her, just an arm and a greenish liquid flying at me. Then I was on the floor, with my eyes on fire." His hand twitched as if he wanted to reach for his face. "I have a vague recollection of you two talking to me, but I couldn't get any words out. It was like something was burning me from the inside."

He coughed again, deeper this time.

"Rest a moment." Sarah laid her hand on his shoulder remembering the churning blackness assaulting him from within. "We can wait."

Peter turned toward her. "You were here, weren't you? When the poison seemed to clear."

Matthias looked up at her with a grateful nod.

"Yes."

"After that, I felt like I could breathe again, peaceful even. But I was so tired I could've slept forever."

"We're very glad you didn't," Jacob said.

"Later, it seemed like I woke up to a bright light, but I wasn't actually awake…"

The high priest straightened. "You had a vision?"

"Yes, and we were all there."

"What did you see?" he whispered.

Peter sank into his pillow and took a slow breath. "I saw a wide stone path splitting into three narrow paths. The one in front of me didn't go far, and I saw myself standing before the doors of the cathedral, the silver scepter in my hand. Then I turned and saw you, Jacob, and Sarah on a path leading into a forest." He turned toward her. "Oh, and Sarah was holding the hand of a little boy."

"Really?" Her hand went to her abdomen, and the unborn child whose hand she would one day hold.

He coughed again. "Jacob, I have some bad news."

He swallowed hard. "What?"

Peter hesitated. "Sarah's brother was with you."

His eyes widened. "Jonah was there?"

"Are you sure it was him?" she asked.

"Average height, brown hair sticking out every which way, obnoxious smirk."

"Sounds about right." Jacob rubbed the stubble on his jaw. "But where exactly were we?"

"I don't know." Peter shook his head, then grimaced in pain. "Somewhere in the mountains, but I didn't recognize the terrain. After that, you disappeared into the forest, and I turned toward a bright light."

"A forest?" Sarah recalled her owns strange visions from her anointing last year. "Did you happen to see a giant tree with leaves tipped with fire?"

"No, and I'd remember that. But father, I saw you on another path bathed in light. You were reaching for a scroll. It began to unroll, and white fire came from the ends."

Like the stained glass in the nave, and the one in the Scroll Room with blood dripping down the priest's hand. Sarah glanced at Jacob, and he seemed to nod in agreement.

"What scroll?" the high priest asked softly.

"The Fourth Scroll. You took it in your hand and then disappeared into the light."

Matthias looked down at his hands. "Are you sure it was the Fourth Scroll?"

"Pretty sure." Peter leaned back on his pillow and coughed again. "Jacob, just when are you going to get around to healing me?"

"About that... I've been trying, but it doesn't seem to be working like usual."

"Then how about you try a little harder?"

"After you rest more."

"Now would be better."

"Oh, all right." Jacob walked to the head of the bed and rested his hand on Peter's head. "*Deus, cura tuam discipulam. Racupera cam animo et corpore.*"

Sarah added her own silent prayer for the living God to restore Peter to health...for her husband's sake as well as his.

Peter felt about his head for the end of the bandage. "Now get this off my face so I can see."

"Wait, let me do it." Jacob supported Peter's head at the base of his neck and slowly unrolled the layers of cloth.

Sarah bit her lip as the soiled bandages revealed patches of dead skin peeling away from a bright red layer beneath. Pustules dotted the inflamed area around his cheekbones and closed eyes. Peter scrunched up his face as if trying to force his swollen eyelids open.

His own eyes brimming with tears, Matthias turned toward the window.

"Given the deathly silence, I assume I don't look so good," Peter said softly.

"You'll be better in time." Jacob waved his hand in front of his brother's eyes as they opened to narrow slits.

"Why is it so dark in here?"

24

EYES TO SEE

The setting sun cast long shadows in the cathedral's entryway as the priests milled about waiting for the Anointing to begin. Jacob was tasked by his father to stick close to Peter in his first public appearance since the attack a week and a half ago. But his presence might be the least welcome, having repeatedly failed to heal his brother's blindness.

Yet another blow had come a few days ago, when Peter received a letter from Cecilia's father informing him that they would not be coming due to the recent violence. But they wished him a full recovery and looked forward to returning to the holy city later in the spring.

Seeing as the Bethulians hadn't parted on best of terms after their daughter's tantrum at the Calling, Jacob wasn't entirely convinced of their sincerity. Thankfully, his father never worked up the nerve to break the news to them about his marriage to Sarah. He wasn't convinced of their trustworthiness either.

Brother James, the son of the chief priest of Taberah, broke away from a small huddle that had been looking their way for the last several minutes. It was an open secret that a few of the priestly orders in distant cities resented the singular authority of the high priest and his eventual successor.

"Uh, sorry to hear about the attack, Peter." He extended his hand in greeting before it occurred to him that Peter couldn't see it.

"James," Jacob shook the hand of his Taberan counterpart. At least he was one of the few visiting priests with the courage to approach his brother and not just whisper behind his back.

"Thanks, James," Peter said flatly.

"Well, it's good to see you." His pale face reddened. "I mean…" Shaking his head, he retreated to his fellow Taberans.

"Yeah, sure."

Their father strode toward the double doors at the front of the cathedral while Brother Augustus issued orders to the priests and students.

Peter lifted his head and followed the path of the flaming silver scepter as their father passed.

"Could you see that?" Jacob whispered. "The Sacred Fire?"

"Kind of…but it just seems hazy, like the moon behind a thick layer of clouds."

"That's progress though."

"A lot of good that's going to do me."

While Brother Augustus organized the priests into two columns, Caleb and another boy handed out unlit torches.

"What am I supposed to do with this?" Peter barked at their cousin. "It's not like I can anoint anyone."

Father snatched the silver-handled torch and placed it in Peter's palm. "You will stand between me and your brother where you belong."

"Why? So people can come see the blind and disfigured priest?"

"Your skin's looking better, and your beard's coming in well," Jacob said, although Peter's skin was still pink and puckered in spots.

His brother dismissed his encouraging assessment with a shake of his head.

"You're the big draw every year, at least among the female population." Jacob clapped him on the shoulder. "Maybe it'll be the same again this year." But there would be some who'd come out just to see Peter's public debut as a man brought low by tragedy.

"Those days are over." Peter dropped the torch to his side. "But I guess they can gawk all they want. It's not like I'll know."

"That's enough." Father lowered his voice. "Remember who you are...a priest of the House of Eleazar and my son. Now act like it."

He turned and nodded to the young priests standing on either side of the immense wooden doors. With a low groan, the doors swung open before them. Father lifted his silver scepter, and the square abruptly quieted as the priests processed out.

"Steps," whispered Jacob, tightening his grip on Peter's arm. "Five."

"I know. I'm not an imbecile."

The priestly procession formed two rows, one on each side of the silver scepter. Pockets of hushed conversation sprang up, and Jacob cringed at the many mentions of his brother's name. Per his father's orders, he helped Peter take his customary place at their father's right. Jacob found the gesture a touching vote of confidence in Peter's future, although one his brother clearly didn't share.

He looked out on the crowded square, careful to stay within a couple feet of Peter in case his balance faltered. Sarah was somewhere in the fading light with her brother, and surrounded by Reliqui Fideles to hide her condition since she insisted on coming to the Anointing.

Soldiers were stationed along the top of the wall, at the Tower Gate, and the back of the square in a reassuring show of strength. Although attendance seemed less than last year, hundreds more gathered on the other side of the wall, denied admittance due to the council's stricter entry requirements. Their newfound emergency powers were a growing source of frustration and resentment for his father, Hannah, and faithful citizens alike.

"In the name of Patrimus," his father's deep voice boomed across the square, "greetings to all who have come from near and far for the Anointing. It was on the first spring solstice of our age that the faithful remnant received this Sacred Fire at their encampment of Havilah."

While his father told of the divine bolt of lightning that delivered the Sacred Fire to Uriel over two thousand years ago, Jacob's gaze drifted to Mount Peniel in the distance. Its impenetrable white peak rose above the shadows of dusk, still glowing with the last rays of sunlight.

That very same Sacred Fire now burned on his father's scepter and would soon be used to anoint the faithful. Apparently, Peter didn't share their reverent awe. Instead, he gripped his unlit torch as if he'd like to bash someone over the head with it.

Good thing he wouldn't be able to see Jonah coming forward to be anointed, since he'd be a prime target for Peter's pent-up wrath. But as excited as Sarah was for Jonah to be anointed, Jacob was still tempted to try and set his hair on fire.

"And the High Priest shall carry this Sacred Fire before you to sanctify the city that is to come." His father glanced over his shoulder at the soaring stone cathedral. "At its peak, you shall build a holy house that will stand forever as a scepter of the living God. And no accursed thing will be found there, for the holy city will be the dwelling place of the Heir to the Sacred Fire and the anointed ones."

Jacob's heart quickened at the secret known only to Reliqui Fideles, that the long-awaited Heir was here tonight among the faithful, only a month away from being born. But might others be present who knew of the prophesied one? Dark spirits and their human allies who would do everything in their unholy power to destroy the baby and his mother?

He scanned the crowd as the choir lined up on the wide steps of the arcade, their opening notes of *Inceptio Novus* rising above the square. In defiance of his fear, Jacob joined the rest of the square in the triumphant song sung from the beginning of the age, one that pointed to the everlasting age to come.

He glanced at Peter, who stood mute, seemingly alone in his misery. For all the Bethulians' talk of honor and family loyalty, abandoning his brother in his time of need struck him as the height of hypocrisy. If anyone needed a new beginning, a renewed reason for living, it was Peter.

"Hold up your torch," Jacob whispered as the song reached its end. "A little higher…"

"Yeah, I got it."

After a solemn pause, their father turned and lowered his blazing scepter to light Peter's torch with the Sacred Fire. As he turned to the priest on his other side, Peter drew a sharp breath, as if he'd taken a blow to the stomach.

"What's the matter?" Jacob lit the end of his own torch from his brother's leaping flame.

His scarred lips formed a smile for the first time since his attack. "I can see."

"What?" Jacob nearly lost his grip on the silver handle.

From his right, Brother Augustus loudly cleared his throat. He reached over to light his torch with a trembling hand.

As the Sacred Fire sped down the line of priests and brightened the square, Jacob turned back to Peter. "What do mean, you can see?"

His brother closed his eyes, brow furrowed. "In my mind's eye, I can see."

25

UNWELCOME VISITORS

Did Peter just smile? Sarah hadn't seen her brother-in-law since he'd first awoken from the attack. Jacob said he'd kept mostly to their quarters since then, sullen and withdrawn, even from his fellow priests. Yet now he stood tall, looking older and wiser with his short beard...and definitely smiling.

Her father-in-law, the high priest, raised his silver scepter. "Come, be anointed as those who have gone before us, that we may be sanctified to do the work prepared for us in our years."

The eager crowd moved forward. Jacob and a couple dozen priests began anointing the faithful. He dipped his fingers in a bronze basin of oil, then passed them through the Sacred Fire on his torch. His fingertips alight, he touched the small flame to the foreheads of each person, and the fire disappeared.

"What are we waiting for?" Jonah asked as those on either side of them shuffled toward the front of the square. "The sooner I get my fire, the sooner I get my feast."

"You can't be serious." Sarah shook her head. "Did you not hear the beautiful story about the giving of the Sacred Fire on the holy mountain?"

"Yeah, but I didn't come for a history lesson."

Grandmother rounded on him. "If you can't demonstrate a little more respect for this holy occasion, I may send you back to the bakery myself. With no dinner," she added as the obvious question formed on Jonah's lips.

That quieted him. But Sarah's stomach had begun to ache too, and the traditional Anointing feast of roasted lamb with all the accompaniments made her mouth water.

With a nod from Grandmother, George took the point position, and they began to press forward. Sarah wore her thick winter cloak, but no amount of Cornelia's skillful tailoring could hide her pregnant state completely. So, George and Marta went in front of her, Jonah and Grandmother on each side of her, and Garth and Clara behind her.

"Let us in," someone shouted from the other side of the wall. "We want to be anointed too."

Sarah lamented the disappointment of the many families they had passed at the Tower Gate. Some must have traveled for days, only to be denied admittance due to a lack of papers they had no idea were required now.

"This is unlawful," another called, drawing the attention of soldiers stationed on the wall.

"They're absolutely right." Grandmother pursed her lips. "It is unlawful and a disgrace that the gate isn't open to all on this holiest of days."

Heads turned toward the sound of scuffling. A smattering of shouts arose, followed by several sharp cracks as if something struck the stone wall.

Based on the vibration behind Sarah's eyes, tempers were flaring.

But one woman stood with her back to the wall, scanning the square. Frizzy red hair protruded from the hood of her cloak, trimmed in jade green.

Sarah ducked behind Jonah, then tugged on Marta's sleeve.

"Isn't that the palm reader over by the wall, directly opposite us?"

She stood on the balls of her feet to see through the crowd. "That's her. I'd know that wild hair and smug face anywhere."

"Did she see you?" Grandmother whispered.

Sarah peered between Jonah and Garth. "I don't think so, but there are several more women spaced out along the wall." She narrowed her eyes. "The mother of the demon child's there too. It looks like her lips are moving."

Fiona materialized beside them. "I don't like this. We should leave now."

"What do you make of those women standing along the wall?" Grandmother asked her. "They're watching the square instead of the chaos behind them."

Fiona drew in a sharp breath. "They're uttering curses."

Sarah's hand went to her temple as a wave of darkness passed over them, bringing with it a subtle anger and instinct to lash out at the disruption.

A loud bang sounded as if something hard struck armor. A company of soldiers charged across the square.

"Watch out," Garth cried as a rock sailed overhead.

More soldiers took up a defensive position at the front of the square. Matthias appeared to be arguing with the commanding officer as his priests continued to anoint the faithful, albeit at a faster pace. Jacob's head bobbed over the crowd, worry etched on his face.

Jonah yelped as a rock thudded into his shoulder. With a burst of rage, he picked it up, preparing to hurl it back from where it came.

"Jonah, no!" Sarah clutched his arm, quelling some of his anger before he jerked his arm away.

"What do you think you're doing?" a nearby soldier growled.

He dropped the rock at his feet. "Nothing."

"The boy was hit with the rock." Grandmother shook a finger in the guard's face. "I suggest you focus on restoring order."

As the stabbing pain behind her eyes worsened, Sarah reached in her cloak for the comfort of her teardrop necklace.

A hideous scream rang out. A young guard on top of the wall swayed, clutching the arrow shot through his neck. With more shouts and screams from those below, he toppled off the wall. The swell of rage from his fellow soldiers almost drove her to her knees.

She looked for Jacob at the front of the square. He shoved his torch at Peter and sprinted toward the fallen soldier.

Panic setting in, the crowd surged every which way. An elderly man fell to the ground with others stumbling over him. Garth waded through the crowd to help him.

"This has to stop," Sarah murmured.

"It's you they're looking for," Grandmother hissed in her ear.

"I know." But one young guard was likely dead and others injured. The faithful were at risk of being trampled.

At the front of the square, Matthias waved his scepter, yelling. "Peace, peace!"

But fear and rage were spreading, the fortunetellers' curses fanning the flames. In their depravity, they'd love nothing more than to see violence spill into the city streets, and to blame the priests for the tragic results.

Her stomach churned at the thought of what her baby might be enduring. The unfolding chaos and hatred were beyond her ability to calm but not beyond the power of the Sacred Fire and the living God himself. This was the work she was sanctified to do, even if it drew the attention of the vile fortunetellers cursing her, cursing all who'd come to be anointed.

As more rocks flew overhead, Sarah crouched low, weaving

through the crowd, away from Grandmother and Marta, who could be recognized. She extended her hand toward the white flame at the front of the square and whispered, "Veni Spiritus Pacis."

Out of the corner of her eye, red flashed as the palm reader's head spun toward her.

With a low roar, the Sacred Fire leapt skyward from the silver scepter. The square became as bright as noon. Sarah spied her nemesis only twenty yards away, just before the spirit of peace sent the palm reader sprawling.

As the cool wind swept over her, the blood and white fire that had been racing through her veins slowed, along with time itself. She longed to stay in that place of peace and solitude, but the exclamations of those in the square intruded.

The heart-shaped face of Fiona came into focus, a flicker of fire in her black pupils. She caught Sarah as her knees wobbled. "Are you hurt?"

"No." She scanned the square, but there didn't seem to be a single fortuneteller left standing.

Fiona helped her back to Grandmother and the others. Somewhere by the wall, Jacob must have been tending to the injured. All around them, people helped strangers get to their feet and dust themselves off.

"George, you have to get Sarah out of here before they regroup." Grandmother patted the gray hairs that had blown loose from her bun. "And take Jonah before he gets himself in any more trouble."

"We need to go toward the Sacred Fire." Sarah looked at the front of the square where the flames had returned to normal size, and the shocked priests were anointing people again. "The fortunetellers won't want to get close to it."

"Especially after that display of might," Garth said, his dark hair disheveled.

"What about the rest of you?" She turned to Marta. "You can't let the palm reader see you."

"We'll head to the back of the square, then cut behind them to the Tower Gate." Grandmother motioned for them to get started. "Meet us at the bakery as soon as possible."

George glanced at his wife.

"I'll be fine, dear." Marta patted his arm. "You stay with the children."

"We're not children," Jonah protested.

"They'll be watching the south gate out of the Heights for a very pregnant woman too," Grandmother whispered.

George grabbed Jonah by the collar. "Fortunately, we don't need a gate."

The three of them fell in behind a family exclaiming over the miracle of the leaping fire and the cessation of the violence and chaos. George kept his arm around Sarah like a protective father, concealing her belly with his bulk.

Just before they reached the priest on the end of the row, he steered them into the heavy flow of foot traffic leaving the square.

"But I didn't get anointed," Jonah grumbled.

Sarah sighed. "Maybe next year."

They turned down the broad promenade, the grand homes of the First Families on one side and expensive inns, restaurants, and shops on the other.

Five minutes later, she rubbed her temple. Even though they were now several blocks from the square, it was still there...a faint simmering anger that wasn't coming from her brother, whose anger had been purged by the peaceful wind. "I think we're being followed."

"Don't turn around," George hissed. "Stay at this pace, and I'll catch up in a moment." He removed his pocket watch and paused beneath one of the oil streetlamps.

"What do they want with you?" Jonah whispered.

"I'm sure they don't like that I'm a peacemaker, but they're really after the baby."

"What? Why?"

"That would require a history lesson."

George drew even with them. "The red headed fortuneteller's a block and a half back. She looks to be alone."

Jonah's hand squeezed into a fist. "What are we going to do?"

"At the next street, we're going to casually turn right."

"Clara said she lived in the tavern district, but she's a long way from there," Sarah whispered as they turned off the promenade.

George nodded. "And she's going in the opposite direction."

They walked a couple more blocks in silence before Sarah said, "I'm not so sure she is following us. I can't feel her as strongly as before."

"Maybe we lost her," George said.

He turned to Jonah. "Slow up here to look in the window of the haberdasher. See if you can catch a glimpse of her."

He puffed out his chest at being assigned a task.

"She just turned the corner," Jonah reported a minute later. "But she's staggering a little, like she's drunk or hurt or something."

"Then she's quite aways back now." George frowned. "If she is following us, it's strange that she's moving so slowly."

The street sloped downward. The high stone wall around the Heights loomed thirty yards ahead. Beyond, a thick haze of chimney smoke hung in the air.

They passed beneath a sign for the Tall Tales Tavern, and George said, "Turn here."

After rounding the corner, they hustled through the main door to the inn attached to the tavern. George moved to the edge of the window that fronted the street. Jonah followed, looking over his shoulder.

Sarah ducked under George's massive arm braced against the wall. The palm reader passed into the circle of lamplight, her red hair sticking out at odd angles and cloak askew. She veered into the street and crossed to the other side.

Sarah gasped. "Look at that sign farther down...Eye of the Soothsayer."

Stars surrounded a sliver of moon and a red eye, slitted like a cat's. The palm reader headed straight for the storefront.

"I'm going to follow her." Jonah turned to the door. "See who else is there."

George clamped a hand on his forearm. "No, you won't."

A black carriage rolled slowly past the window, blocking their view.

"I don't believe it." A vein bulged on George's thick neck.

Sarah peered at the shiny coach with a fancy red A on the door. A chill passed through her, and she whispered, "Arcanus?"

George pulled them away from the window. "We're done here." He led them toward the bespectacled innkeeper dozing behind the counter.

"Not a peep out of you." He gave Jonah a menacing glance.

The innkeeper jolted awake at their approach. "A room, sir?"

"Two rooms. Adjoining, please." George placed a gold Meriban medallion on the stained wooden counter.

Sarah's eyes widened at the exorbitant sum.

"Ah, very good." The proprietor pocketed the shiny coin.

An assortment of keys hung on pegs behind him. He removed a rusty iron key ring from the far end of the counter.

"But George," Sarah whispered. "Everyone will be frantic with worry if we stay here tonight."

"I know."

"And what about the feast?" Jonah asked. "These rooms

should come with dinner seeing as how much you paid for them."

"Can you two just be quiet?" Sweat glistened on his bald head.

"This way, please." The innkeeper gave Sarah a sideways glance. Did a tiny white flame flicker in his black pupils, or was it the reflection of his candle?

They followed him toward a broad wooden staircase. But instead of climbing it to the rooms above, they continued past the noisy kitchen to a hall at the back of the inn.

"Enjoy your stay." The innkeeper unlocked a door at the end of the hall and handed George the stub of a candle.

He nodded and shooed them into the room.

"What a dump." Jonah crinkled his nose at the moldy smell and the two low beds with straw mattresses.

Sarah rubbed her arms. It would be a cold night with no fireplace and one thin blanket atop each bed.

George handed her the candle, then opened the doors of a wardrobe.

"I thought you got two rooms," Jonah said.

"I did." He stepped aside. "Now in you go."

Sarah lowered the candle and peered at the square opening at the back of the wardrobe.

"Oh, maybe I'll get dinner after all." Jonah scrambled through first.

She passed him the sputtering candle, then crawled on her hands and knees through the wardrobe and over a section of rough rock. George followed, then lowered the false back of the wardrobe, leaving the Heights behind.

Jonah helped Sarah to her feet in a dusty storeroom with broken chairs, tables, and stacks of linens on shelves. George looked longingly at the casks of ale as they hurried past and out the door. Then they weaved their way through a crowded tavern where the patrons appeared in a peaceful mood.

Twenty minutes later, they reached the bakery. In the front hallway, Sarah fell into Jacob's waiting arms while Grandmother pulled Jonah into a fierce embrace.

Marta kissed George's cheek. "Well done, dear."

"Is everyone else all right?" Sarah clung to her husband.

"Yes," Grandmother replied. "Thank heaven, everyone is accounted for now."

Jonah peered into the dining room at the empty place settings. "We're still going to have the feast, right?"

Sarah raised her eyebrows. "That's what you're concerned about at the moment?"

Her brother looked to George for support.

"I could do with a bite to eat myself."

"Then it'll be dry lamb and mushy vegetables." Marta headed for the kitchen. "But Jonah, if you want to eat, you'd better come help me."

"Let's wait by the fire." Grandmother waved the rest of them into the parlor.

Sarah flopped down on the coach. "Oh, it feels so good to get off my feet."

"I think you need a foot rub after all that walking." Jacob slipped off her shoes.

She stretched out on the sofa with her stockinged feet on his lap.

Grandmother smiled at her. "I assume your return from the Heights went smoothly then."

Sarah glanced over her belly at George. "Not exactly."

Grandmother's smile faded. "What happened?"

"I thought we were being followed down the promenade by the palm reader, but it turned out she was just headed in the same direction as us."

Jacob tensed, squeezing her foot extra hard.

"We ducked into the Tall Tales Tavern and watched her go by," George said.

"She was headed for a storefront called Eye of the Soothsayer," Sarah said. "It had a sign with the cat's eye and stars, like the other fortunetellers."

Grandmother drew in a sharp breath. "Fiona said that after the fortunetellers in the square recovered their wits, about half of them headed toward the promenade."

"Maybe the Eye of the Soothsayer is a gathering place for them," Sarah suggested.

"Did you see any others enter the building?" Jacob abandoned her foot massage.

Sarah sat up. "No, but a huge coach with a red A was headed there as well."

"What?" Grandmother's hand went to her mouth. "An Arcanus... Which one?"

"There was only one passenger, but I couldn't get a clear look," George said. "Don't think he was big enough to be Sylvaneus though."

"Niccolus?"

"Could be."

Grandmother's brow furrowed. "The involvement of the Arcanus clan is never a good sign."

"No," George shifted his weight. "But at least we have an idea where the fortunetellers might be meeting."

"That could prove useful." Grandmother turned to Jacob. "I'm very curious what your father will make of this evening's developments."

"If tonight doesn't change his mind about Sarah and our baby, I don't know what will."

26

RECONVENING THE REMNANT

The following evening, under the cover of darkness, Goran's carriage rolled to a stop in front of Thaniel's house. With a nod from Grandmother, George got out first then offered his hand to Sarah. In her state, there was no way to disembark both gracefully and quickly, so she chose the latter. Grandmother was right behind her.

As they approached the front door, Thaniel's anxious face peeked through the draperies. He greeted them in the front hallway, then sent Sarah to the kitchen, which smelled of freshly baked cinnamon cookies.

Cornelia seemed to be scolding Demetrius. "Since you're here, do let me measure you for a proper coat. The cut of this one is all wrong for your build."

"Thank you, but this one serves me well," he said.

She shook her finger at him. "Why must you insist on looking shabby?"

Fiona gave Sarah a little wave and looked like she was trying not to laugh at Demetrius's plight.

His black brows furrowed. "There are times I'd prefer not to look like a soldier, tonight being one of them."

Cornelia reached for Fiona's hand. "How can you stand to be seen with him?"

She gave a mock sigh. "We all have our burdens to bear."

"In certain circles, shabby is a good way to blend in," Garth said from the kitchen table.

Cornelia rounded on him. "And your coat smells of ale, so I think we know what circles you've been traveling in."

He chuckled. "Men get loose tongues after a couple tankards of ale, which can help our cause."

"Oh, hello, Sarah." Cornelia shooed Garth aside so Sarah could sit at the kitchen table. "Care for a cookie?"

Grandmother and Thaniel joined them, with George left behind to keep watch out front.

"We shouldn't linger long," Grandmother said. "But our enemies made their presence known at the Anointing, so perhaps we can we learn from that."

"Fi told me the fortunetellers showed up, but I was on the other side of the wall with my hands full at the time." A purple bruise shaded Demetrius's jaw.

"We estimate there were at least ten stationed around the square, including the two Sarah recognized."

"But that leaping fire sure drove them away." Garth reached for a cookie.

Demetrius gave Sarah an admiring nod. "I figured it was you since I doubted Matthias could pull that off.

"It really wasn't me at all." No, she had been weak and overwhelmed, yet blessed with a powerful gift from above.

"Unfortunately, the palm reader recognized Sarah, so we had to split up with George taking Sarah and Jonah down the promenade, then doubling back to one of his unofficial exits," Grandmother said.

Demetrius straightened. "Jonah should not be slinking around the Heights. He looks so much like Thaddeus that if Niccolus Arcanus ever lays eyes on him, this ruse is over."

"I know that." Grandmother sounded more annoyed with herself than Demetrius. "He won't set foot in the Heights again until we get to the bottom of this situation, and maybe not even then. But it gets worse."

She motioned for Sarah to continue. "We thought the palm reader was following us, but it turned out she was going to a place called Eye of the Soothsayer in the west end of the Heights."

"Sounds like fortune telling for the well-heeled," Thaniel said.

"The sign for the establishment had golden stars and a red eye, slitted like a cat's eye."

"I've never really liked cats," Garth said to no one in particular.

"Then it must have some connection to the fortunetellers we've already identified," Demetrius said.

Grandmother cleared her throat. "This is the part where it gets worse."

"While we were hiding in a tavern, a black carriage pulled up to the Eye of the Soothsayer." Sarah twisted her hands. "It had a red A on the door."

His face darkened. "The House of Arcanus."

"We think there was only one man in the carriage, but we couldn't get a good look at him."

Demetrius rubbed his brow. "Let's pray he didn't get a good look at you or your brother either."

"We should have the place watched," Fiona said. "We might be able to learn something useful based on who's coming and going."

"I agree, and George will arrange that," Grandmother said, "but tell us how the riot started."

Demetrius flexed his swollen hand. "There was a crowd of a few hundred congregating around the Tower Gate, some demanding to be let in. A few got testy with the guards after being turned away, but no one was threatening violence. It seemed we had the situation well in hand, but suddenly rocks started flying, and some troublemakers began trying to push through the gate. As soon as one of our guards on the wall was shot through with an arrow, things spiraled out of control."

"But surely this was an organized effort to draw Sarah out, not a spontaneous riot," Grandmother said.

"You're right about that." Demetrius ran a hand over his beard. "We captured one of the young rock throwers, and I got him to talk. It wasn't even that hard after Sarah did whatever it was she did."

"She called forth the spirit of peace, is what." Garth patted her shoulder, then reached for another cookie.

"Well, the aggressive fool turned pretty docile. Maybe it was the first real peace he'd experienced in years. But he told me he'd been hired to take part in the protests at the Tower Gate and start the violence when the singing ended."

"Hired?" Grandmother exclaimed. "By whom?"

"He insisted he didn't know, and I'm inclined to believe him. He said a well-dressed woman struck up a conversation with him and his drinking friends in the tavern and paid them to start the riot. And she threatened him with a curse if he backed out."

"Oh, dear. I don't care for all this business with curses." Cornelia's hand trembled as she nibbled on a cookie.

"But what is the connection between these fortunetellers and the House of Arcanus?" Thaniel asked.

"I don't know." Grandmother sighed. "We must be missing something."

"They'd both like to see the House of Eleazar weakened," he suggested. "And they have no love for the House of Magdala either, since both have historically thwarted their ambitions."

"True." Grandmother scowled. "And the Arcanus clan will exploit any weakness or tragedy, like Peter's attack, to consolidate their power. But I find it hard to believe they'd dabble in the occult."

"And yet, years ago, Niccolus pronounced a Triatus curse on Thaddeus," Demetrius said. "But why? That's the question that haunts me."

Fiona looked up at him with tenderness, as if she had a past that haunted her too.

But Sarah shuddered. What kind of person cursed a man in his dying moments?

"We know he saw Argus set fire to your house with your mother and grandmother inside since...um, a witness saw him there. And Argus was a constant embarrassment to the House of Arcanus, prone to drinking, fighting, and frequenting brothels." Demetrius shook his head. "Yet apparently still his father's favorite."

Grandmother steepled her hands. "I know you have your own theory as to what happened that night."

His dark eyes flitted to Sarah, then back to Grandmother who gave him a slight nod.

"It's more than a theory. I just could never prove it," he growled. "When I tracked down Thaddeus, he was already dead in the street. Argus looked like he was trying to say something with his dying breath, yet instead of comforting his brother and receiving his last words, Niccolus jumped to his feet to loudly pronounce a curse on a dead man. Sorry, Sarah. I don't mean to upset you."

"You think Niccolus killed his brother Argus after he killed my father," Sarah said.

"It's the only plausible explanation. The blade that pierced his heart was expensive, encrusted with jewels. Your father would never have carried such a pretentious weapon, even if he could've afforded it. The angle of the entry wound didn't make sense either. But with the holy city descending into chaos, no one was interested in such details."

"Niccolus became the sole heir of the House of Arcanus that night," Grandmother said.

Garth muttered a few choice words about his cousin's killer.

Thaniel nodded. "So, in his supposed fury, he pronounced the curse as a distraction from his own murderous deed."

Her face taut, Grandmother turned to Fiona. "What can you tell us about the Triatus curse?"

"It's thought to be a powerful blood curse that endures for three generations. Soothsayers and sorcerers believe that just before he was defeated, Kadmiel cursed the land, and it still retains traces of his power." She hesitated, as if she didn't want to give voice to the profane practices of her past life. "They draw on that dark power of the first age to cast their spells and curses."

Sarah stiffened on the hard chair. Was that the low vibration she could sense at times? A residue of Kadmiel's rage that could be used by fortunetellers and their ilk for dark purposes?

"Hogwash." Garth waved away the disturbing theory.

"We'd certainly like to believe that," said Grandmother, her face grim.

"But if Niccolus Arcanus is the murderer I think he is, and he's working with these fortunetellers, then we've got an even bigger problem on our hands." Demetrius crossed his arms over his chest. "I don't see a way around it. Sarah should leave the city...and soon."

Dread exploded in her chest at the thought of leaving all these people who'd become so dear. Family by blood, faith, and shared trials.

"They staged an attack inside the cathedral, and who's to say they can't do it again," he added.

Sarah couldn't fault the gruff captain who remained loyal to her father's memory, and his family, more than fifteen years after his murder. But how could she leave Grandmother and Jonah? And how could Jacob leave his teaching, his brother and father, and the only home he'd ever known?

There had to be another way.

27

VESSEL OF FIRE

The evening prayer service on wisdom and discernment was the shortest Jacob could remember.

As confused students and teachers filed out of the nave, his father whispered. "Meet me in my study in ten minutes. Bring your brother."

Peter was never one to linger in the hallowed stillness after evening prayers. But he'd had a change of heart since discovering several nights ago at the Anointing that he could see while in close proximity to the Sacred Fire. Head bowed, he sat on the front row, apparently taking matters into his own hands given that Jacob's prayers had failed him thus far.

When the footsteps and voices in the hallway gave way to several minutes of silence, Jacob tapped his brother on the shoulder.

"What?"

"Father wants to see us."

"Why?"

"I don't know."

He rose with a huff and headed for the door in the north

transept, his gait less steady as they moved farther from the Sacred Fire.

"Good, you're both here." Their father rose from his desk.

"You wanted to speak with us?" Peter didn't bother disguising his irritation.

"Yes, but not here." He lowered his voice. "The time has come to visit the Scroll Room."

Jacob's gaze fell to the floor, as if he could see through it to the hidden room beneath their feet. "For the Fourth Scroll?"

"That remains to be seen," Father said.

Jacob crept down the back hallway ahead of them, checking for any students who had disobeyed strict orders to remain in their dormitory after prayers. But the passage was as silent as a tomb.

Their father opened the broom closet door, which appeared ready to fall off its hinges. The smell of mold and dust was enough to dissuade anyone from entering. "Keep a lookout while I open the inner door."

"Clearly that falls to you, Jacob." Peter leaned against the gray stone, his arms crossed over his chest.

While Father searched for the hidden keyhole in the mortar, Jacob's mind whirled with questions. Did his father finally believe that Sarah was carrying the Heir to the Sacred Fire? And did he recognize the threats to Sarah and the baby from their many enemies? Would he help keep them safe now, as he'd done for Sarah and Jonah as young children?

"Come on." Father waved them into the closet.

And, most importantly, what answers would the Fourth Scroll hold as to the coming days, months, and years of their lives?

Peter shuffled forward, his foot catching on an old bucket.

"Careful," Father said as the clanging reverberated down the hallway.

"A little to your right." Jacob guided his brother toward the secret staircase at the back of the closet.

His hands in front of him, Peter felt for the opening. "Oh, gross." He shook off a cobweb and wiped his hand on his robe.

"Watch your head."

"How am I supposed to do that? It's not like I have a flaming torch of the Sacred Fire."

"Duck," Jacob said just before his brother's head scraped the doorframe.

"Ow." Peter rubbed the top of his head. "A little more precision would be nice."

"I'm sorry."

"You should be," he snarled.

Jacob suspected that statement had more to do with his inability to restore his brother's sight than his bumping his head just now.

Father closed the outer closet door. "Help Peter down the stairs while I lock the door."

"I'll go first." Jacob squeezed past him on the stone landing.

Peter extended his hand, feeling along on the wall with his fingertips. Partway down the curving staircase he stopped, his face scrunched in concentration.

"What's wrong?" Jacob reached for his forearm as he swayed slightly.

"Get off me." Peter swatted his hand away. "I can see."

"What?"

He pointed to the faint light of the Sacred Fire at their feet. "I can see in my mind again." His hand at his side, he followed Jacob down the stairs, pushing past him when they reached the bottom.

In the center of the circular room, the Sacred Fire burned low and calm on a slender olive branch in a silver stand. Peter stood a foot away from the white flame as though it were a balm for his troubled soul.

The light was too dim for Jacob to make out Obadiah's visions painted on the plaster walls, but he knew they were there. Beautiful and disturbing, they told of days yet to come. As to when and how, he prayed the Fourth Scroll held some answers.

Their father entered the room, and the flame swirled higher. Then a section of wall beneath the staircase began to shimmer. In the next instant, a rectangular portion turned into a pane of clear glass. Behind it, scrolls and other objects appeared on glass shelves. The flickering firelight played on the crystal cabinet, making it seem like it had no back and no end to its mysteries.

Petite et aperietur vobis glimmered in silver script on the smooth glass surface.

"Ask and the door shall be opened to you," Jacob murmured.

His father stroked his beard. "Now, let's see if we truly have need of the Fourth Scroll."

Peter joined them, his earthly eyes closed.

"I, Matthias son of Mordecai, High Priest and servant of the living God, stand at the door and humbly ask that it be opened to me."

The glass rippled as though a tiny pebble had been dropped into a pond. Then it vanished altogether.

Jacob stared at the Fourth Scroll a few feet in front of them. Pristine white, its silver leaf seal was untarnished by the two millennia it had lain next to the other three Sacred Scrolls that formed the foundation of their faith.

"What's that?" Peter pointed to a small silver container on the shelf above the scrolls. "The egg-shaped thing?"

"That's strange…" Jacob didn't remember it being there a few weeks ago when he came to request the necklace for Sarah from almost the same spot.

"It's a Vasignis," their father said.

Jacob leaned closer, his hands on his knees. "A vessel of fire…"

"That's how the fire bearers of old carried the Sacred Fire on their travels. But don't touch—"

Peter reached for the silver oval and pulled it from the cabinet. "How does it work?"

Father frowned. "I told you not to touch it."

He twisted the top half, and it popped off in his hand.

"What are you doing?" Jacob asked as his brother pivoted toward the Sacred Fire.

Their father lunged after him. "Be careful—"

Jacob held his breath as Peter's hand passed through the flame.

When he removed it unchanged, tiny tongues of white flame peaked over the edge of the silver cup on his palm.

His scarred face alight with hope, Peter snapped the lid back in place. "If I could carry the Sacred Fire with me at all times, I'd be almost normal again."

"Look, it has words." Jacob stepped closer, trying to make out the intricate white letters now visible around the middle of the Vasignis. "*Sicut sanguis ad sanguinem, ignis ad ignem vocat*…as blood calls to blood, fire calls to fire."

"Can I keep it?" Peter clutched the strange object to his chest.

If the answer was no, Jacob was certain it would take both of them to wrestle it away from his brother.

"For now, anyway." Father nodded. "But let's keep this matter to ourselves."

"Yeah, let our enemies think I'm totally blind." Peter's mouth formed a hard line.

Their father took a deep breath. "But now the question is, do we have a genuine need to open the Fourth Scroll?"

Jacob turned to him. "Of course, we do."

"What if the cabinet opened for Peter's sight?"

"But we came here for the Fourth Scroll."

"Did we?" His father's eyes flitted to the crystal cabinet.

The glass door had returned, and the glimmering letters were beginning to fade.

"No!" Jacob's hand jerked toward the scroll but met solid glass. The object that could hold the key to his family's future was once more out of reach.

"Now you've done it," Peter said.

Tongues of fire leapt from the flaming olive branch as if in a holy rebuke.

"I'm sorry. I don't know what I was thinking." Jacob backed away from the cabinet. His throbbing hand was not the one ordained to take hold of the Fourth Scroll.

"Maybe we got what we needed." Peter cradled the Vasignis. "Maybe this is the answer to our prayers."

"But we still need to know what's in the Fourth Scroll."

With a heavy sigh, their father turned his back on the fading crystal cabinet and moved a few paces to stand in front of the Sacred Fire. "Leave me."

"What?" Jacob peered at him.

"Get out, both of you." He wiped a bead of sweat from his brow. "I can't think or pray with all your bickering."

"But the Fourth Scroll—"

"Go." He pointed to the stairs.

Jacob shoved Peter toward the staircase.

"I don't know why you're mad at me." Peter leapt up the stairs two at a time.

"If you weren't so self-absorbed, we'd have—"

"Oh, because I wanted to see again."

"Just shut up." Jacob's fist clenched, tempted as he was to grab his brother by his robe and hurl him back down the stairs.

Instead, he stopped halfway up the staircase to put some distance between the two of them before he got himself in even more trouble. Neither the flame nor his wife would approve of any violence.

His father stood before the Sacred Fire, his head bowed. Across from him, Obadiah's painting of a priest reaching for a scroll appeared on the pale plaster wall, a shiny trickle of blood on his outstretched hand.

28

———

THE SILVER SEAL

Jacob leaned against the wall outside his father's study, tapping his foot on the stone floor.

"What do you think it means?" Peter asked.

"I don't know." Jacob glanced down the hallway where a single torch cast flickering shadows. "But he's been down there almost an hour, so that can't be good."

"No, not Father." Peter shoved the gleaming silver oval in his face. "The saying on the Vasignis...as blood calls to blood, fire calls to fire. Why is it there?"

Jacob pushed off the wall. "I don't know, and right now, I don't care. I'm much more interested in what we came for."

Peter scowled. "Well, then you can wait up. I'm going to bed."

He strode down the hall and nearly collided with their father as he came around the corner...empty handed.

"See you both in the morning." Peter said with a half-hearted wave.

"Wait." Father glanced at the empty passage. "In my study..."

"Sorry about our behavior earlier." Jacob followed him into the north turret, trying to gauge his expression.

"Close the door," his father called over his shoulder.

"Yeah, sorry about that little fight Jacob started." Peter shut the door behind them. "I was pretty excited about being able to see again."

"As we all should be. But now we have another task before us." He removed a small scroll from the sleeve of his robe and placed it on his desk.

"Is that the Fourth Scroll?" Jacob leaned over the dark wood.

"Yes, bring the lamp."

He grabbed an oil lamp from the stand behind the desk.

Peter inched closer. "Now what?"

Taking a deep breath, their father picked up the scroll and examined the silver seal in the lamplight. He slid his thumb under the edge that had begun to pull away after so many centuries of waiting.

The faint aroma of myrrh and sandalwood greeted them as silvery gray vapors arose from the seal. A few moments later, the seal disintegrated entirely.

"That's a good sign, right?" Jacob whispered.

Staring at the scroll, his father nodded. "I would think so."

"At least none of us were incinerated," Peter said.

Jacob's eyes widened. "It's opening."

Rays of light streamed from the ends of the scroll as it began to unroll. With trembling hands, Father straightened the glowing parchment, the white light giving his face a timeless and luminescent appearance.

He looked up at them, his pupils mere pinpricks. "It's written in fire."

In the next instance, Peter clapped his hands over his ears and fell to his knees.

"What's wrong?" Jacob bent over him.

Father set the scroll down and the light faded, leaving his face crinkled with confusion. "What happened?" He hurried around his wide desk.

"Didn't you hear that?" Peter choked out.

Jacob pulled him to his feet. "Hear what?"

"That roar of rage." Peter shuddered. "It seemed like it passed right through me."

"Rage?" Jacob looked to the door. "Oh, no…Sarah."

"You'd better go." Peter clutched his head. "Quickly!"

SARAH MASSAGED her low back as she waited for her herbal tea to steep. While the calming drink would help her fall asleep, it also meant she'd have to visit the bathroom a few hours later. At eight and a half months pregnant, she longed for her body to return to its former proportions and hold in her arms the miraculous little body growing within her.

Despite the late hour, Grandmother sat at the kitchen table nursing her own cup of tea. Since the Anointing, she'd hardly left Sarah's side, which both comforted and saddened her. Left unspoken in the last couple days was the belief shared by everyone in Reliqui Fideles, aside from her and Jacob, that she needed to leave the city for her own safety and her baby's.

She glanced around the tidy kitchen. Tears threatened just thinking about leaving her home of the last two years, her beloved grandmother, sweet Marta and George, and the holy city. Besides, Jacob was utterly opposed to her being more than twenty minutes away at any time, so terrified was he of his own tragic history repeating.

Grandmother had suggested her exile was only until Peter's attacker could be caught and they identified the nefarious sect of fortunetellers and their malevolent schemes. And she'd try to convince Matthias to send Jacob away under some pretext so he could secretly join her. Demetrius promised they'd figure out the connection to the House of Arcanus and how to defend against it.

Just as Sarah reached for her herbal tea, an unseen blast of hatred slammed into her like a massive fist, knocking the breath from her lungs. The room reeled, her tea cup slipped from its saucer, and Grandmother screamed.

Then she lay on her side in warm wet liquid. She sucked in a breath of air again, along with the scent of chamomile. Tea, it was only tea soaking into the wool rug beneath her.

"What happened?" Grandmother fell to her knees beside her. "Sarah, what's wrong?"

She looked into her grandmother's blurred face as more questions came fast and frantic.

A man called her name through thundering footsteps on the stairs. The cellar door burst open. Then Jacob was kneeling beside her, reaching for her wrist, feeling for her pulse.

His hands ran over her abdomen, praying a healing prayer. Sarah grimaced as the baby kicked her in the bladder. For once, she was grateful.

Jacob bent his face close to hers. "Can you hear me?"

She managed a slight nod.

He took her hand. "Just rest and breathe...and remember the fire that burns within you."

Grandmother rubbed her back, whispering prayers of her own.

"How did you know?" Sarah asked in a hoarse voice.

"Peter felt it too...when the Fourth Scroll was opened."

Grandmother gasped. "Your father finally relented."

Jacob helped Sarah sit up. "Yes, we went to the Scroll Room after evening prayers, but something strange happened when the seal was broken."

More footsteps sounded, and Peter appeared in the cellar doorway. "Is Sarah all right?"

"Yes." Jacob nodded. "The baby too."

"Good, because Father wants you to come quickly...all of you."

Peter turned and sped down the stairs.

"For heaven's sake, be careful," Grandmother called after him.

"He'll be fine." Jacob helped Sarah to her feet. "He can see now."

"What? You finally healed him?"

"No, the Sacred Fire did, in a way."

After Sarah rested at the kitchen table for a few more minutes, they began a slow walk through the tunnel with Jacob recounting his visit to the Scroll Room, Peter finding the Vasignis and becoming a present-day Fire Bearer, and the unsealing of the Fourth Scroll.

"HAVE YOU READ THE SCROLL, FATHER?" Jacob asked when they were safely inside the high priest's study with the door locked.

"Only the very beginning, but you'll soon understand why I wanted you all here. Are you well, Sarah?"

She nodded as they approached his desk, the lovely aroma of fine incense leading the way.

"Please sit." Matthias gestured for Sarah and Hannah to take the two chairs in front of his desk.

Jacob stood behind her, his hand on her shoulder. Peter leaned against a bookshelf, clutching his strange silver egg.

Matthias took a deep breath and unrolled the parchment written over two thousand years before. His face shone, as if standing before the Sacred Fire itself.

"Greetings and honor to the high priest whose hand has broken the silver seal, and to the steadfast sons of Eleazar, the exalted mother, and the faithful steward."

Sarah turned and met Grandmother's astonished gaze. Somehow they were all here together in this place and time as the living God intended. She reached for Jacob's hand as his father continued.

HOLY AND BELOVED, you have been appointed to receive the words of the Fourth Scroll. I am Uriel, and I stand in the presence of the living God. It is he who spoke this message on the mountain top, and he alone knows the time and place of its revealing.

With the unsealing of this scroll, the final chapter of Aclesia's second age begins. For the babe in the mother's womb is the one promised from the dawn of the age, the last Son of Eleazar, the High Priest of the third and everlasting age.

Long have the faithful awaited the coming of the Heir to the Sacred Fire, but so has another. The evil and rebellious one stirs beneath the Desolate Plains. For he too awaits the appearing of the one who would dispossess him of his realm.

As in the days of old, his most potent weapon shall be deceit, and his dark schemes shall plague the land. His followers are within the city gates, and they seek the blood of the child. You will know them by their bitter fruits of deception, desecration, and death. No light dwells within them, for they hate all that is good and true.

But the Faithful Remnant shall be the child's shield as he grows in stature, power, and wisdom. In a secret sanctuary, a hidden host awaits his appearing. Among them dwells the keeper of his weapon, a sword of might beyond mortal imagining. Forged in the fires of creation, the Teleos Sword contains a power his adversary can neither comprehend nor possess. With it he can break the bonds of betrayal, and cut the cords of Kadmiel which strangle all of creation.

As the time of choosing draws near, I will raise up a

watchman on the wall to sound the warning, and I will lift up a voice in the hill country to call to those who wander in darkness. All would do well to heed their words, for a day is coming that has never been seen before and shall never be seen again. Behold, a day of fire will dawn, a fire that searches hearts and minds, a fire from which no one can hide. The wicked and faithless will be consumed by their own desecrating deeds. But my Faithful Remnant I will refine in the Sacred Fire until they become as pure silver, made ready to receive their full inheritance.

This is the pronouncement of Patrimus spoken to his servant Uriel atop the holy mountain. Bind up these words in your hearts, for they were written not with ink but with the spirit of the living God. When you call upon it, that same spirit will guide you in the difficult days to come. Lastly, I exhort you and your fellowship to hold fast to your faith and remember that which is hidden will be revealed.

MATTHIAS LOWERED THE SCROLL, and the white light faded.

Sarah's thoughts churned in the stunned silence, until Peter pointed to the scroll.

"It's changing."

She blinked as her eyes adjusted to the dim lamplight. The parchment seemed to yellow and wrinkle in the high priest's hands.

"It's blank." Matthias looked down at the ancient scroll. "The words have disappeared."

"What?" Jacob raced around the desk.

"I hope someone got all that because you know I didn't," Peter said.

"Quick, give me some paper." Jacob reached for the pen and inkwell on his father's desk.

"Here. You sit." Matthias rummaged through a side drawer and removed a sheaf of paper.

Jacob dipped the pen in ink and began to scribble furiously, pausing only to confer with his father looking over his shoulder.

"Kadmiel is alive," Grandmother murmured.

"That must be who we heard earlier." Peter glanced at Sarah.

She rubbed her temple. "Somehow I think I already knew that."

"He must have sent the versarius after you last year." Grandmother shuddered. "And now we must contend with these despicable fortunetellers and the Seer, whoever that is."

Sarah laid her hand on her bulging belly, and a tiny heel pressed into her palm. Those who would destroy this precious life before it even began were near, within the holy city's gates. And when his life began, what would it hold besides a mysterious sword and an incomprehensible task?

And where was this secret sanctuary with a hidden host? She had no earthly idea, but there was no denying the truth any longer because the living God had decreed it himself. Sooner or later, she and her son would have to leave the holy city, possibly for good.

29

MAYHEM IN THE SQUARE

Hannah twisted her wedding ring under the marble table. What she wouldn't give for her late husband Bartholomew's steady advice now. The Fourth Scroll said Kadmiel's followers were within the city gates, but might they be in this chamber as well? As she'd learned through the years, some of her fellow councilors excelled at deception, especially the one who headed this leadership body.

Sylvaneus Arcanus had already kept them waiting fifteen minutes. While he did like to make an entrance, he was rarely this late. Across from her, Matthias drummed his fingers on the table, no doubt anxious for their dinner meeting later to discuss how to get Sarah and Jacob safely and secretly into hiding.

"Father, how is your son, Peter?" Councilor Miranda broke the silence. "Has he recovered his sight?"

Matthias stirred. "He can perceive light and darkness, but his old eyesight is lost forever. I'm certain he will never be the same."

"Your younger boy couldn't heal him then?" Sebastian asked as someone on the periphery of the chamber snickered.

Matthias stroked his beard. "Apparently, it wasn't to be."

"What could that be a sign of...brotherly enmity? Jealousy?" asked Niccolus from beneath the red and black banner of the House of Arcanus.

Several council members laughed dutifully at the slight.

"Maybe there's a usurper in the House of Eleazar," Niccolus suggested. "What does your Priestly Codex have to say about blind priests?"

Matthias's face hardened. "I'm confident Peter will be able to carry out his duties, now and in the future, despite his impaired sight."

Sylvaneus and Commander Xavier appeared in the doorway of the chamber, and the laughter died.

"Apologies," Sylvaneus grunted, apparently irritated before they had even begun.

After calling the meeting to order, he smoothed his silver hair and announced, "Obviously, we must address the rampant criminality that occurred at the Anointing."

Hannah caught Matthias's eye for a fleeting moment before he turned to face the false accusations and misrepresentations likely coming his way.

"That was a clever trick you used to divert attention in the square," Xavier said. "But many of the holy city's residents were terrified the city was about to burn down."

Several Arcanus allies nodded in agreement, although Hannah had heard no such concerns in her travels around the city in the last few days.

"And the more foolish residents are carrying on about it being a sign from above," Sylvaneus said with a sneer.

"How do you explain the fireball from your scepter?" Xavier trained his hard eyes on the high priest. "What alchemy produced such a reaction?"

Fireball? Hannah shook her head. It seemed a bit early in the meeting for such hyperbole. And the commander only wanted to know in case he could create such a weapon for himself.

"You seem to think I can use the Sacred Fire to do as I wish." Matthias folded his hands on the table. "I assure you, that is not the case for me or any priest. But peace was restored, thankfully."

"Restored after considerable upset and violence, including the loss of a young guard's life. Given our city's tragic fire fifteen years ago, I'd have thought you'd be more sensitive...and repentant," Niccolus said solemnly.

Hannah wanted to slap the false sincerity off his pointed face. Thanks to his brother's despicable actions at the time, she'd lost her daughter and son-in-law, and her grandchildren were left orphaned.

Matthias didn't dignify the comment with a response. While he was doing an admirable job maintaining his composure, she doubted it would last much longer. Hers was thinning too, for that matter.

"Wouldn't it be more productive to hear from Commander Xavier about how the riot started?" she asked.

"Yes, and how his soldiers lost control of the situation in such short order," Matthias added.

A vein pulsed in the commander's wide neck. "And perhaps why your son didn't even attempt to heal my wounded soldier."

Hannah shook her head. The poor boy was probably dead before he hit the ground, and they were wasting precious time with this spat.

"Wasn't he shot through the neck?" Miranda asked. "That's a grievous wound no physician could heal."

Matthias straightened. "My son is a gifted healer, but he can't be expected to raise the dead."

"He practically brought Jedidiah back from the dead last month." Niccolus pointed to the white-haired councilor seated next to Hannah.

"What's that?" Jedidiah cupped a hand over his ear, his hearing just as bad as before.

Sylvaneus banged his hand on the table. "Commander Xavier, your report, please."

"This was not entirely a peaceful gathering of believers who wanted to listen to the Anointing service. Some organized a protest against the gate closure with the intention to commit violence."

"Yes, what do we know about the stone throwing thugs who started the conflict at the Anointing and tried to break through the gate?" asked one of Niccolus's sycophants.

"Their subversive behavior must be punished," another Arcanus ally demanded.

"Yes, but who are they, and where did they come from?" Miranda pressed.

"From what we can tell, they're believers who wanted to attend the Anointing but didn't have the appropriate papers." The commander's lip curled. "Rest assured, they will be punished."

Hannah caught Matthias's eye. So Xavier elected not to share the information they had gleaned from Demetrius about the perpetrators being recruited from local taverns. Instead, they were portrayed as faithful members of Matthias's flock.

The commander cleared his throat. "In my judgment—"

"Why should we be confident in your judgment when Brother Peter's attacker is still at large, chaos unfolded at the Anointing, and people were injured right under your nose?" Miranda shook a petite finger at him.

"However one may feel about the Anointing ceremony and the procedures at the gates, it's bad for business to have visitors and citizens of the holy city injured," Sebastian added.

Hannah glanced out the window across from her and sighed at the fading light. Unfortunately, this was shaping up to be a long meeting, and their all-important dinner discussion would have to wait.

SARAH SAT in a dark corner on the back row of the nave, her empty breadbasket beside her in case anyone questioned why she was in the cathedral. Of course, she had to hold it in front of her belly to try to hide her pregnant state, since only Caleb and Brother Augustus were privy to the knowledge of her marriage to Jacob. But not even they knew that the Fourth Scroll had been opened and that she carried the prophesied Heir.

The Sacred Fire burned low on the silver scepter at the front. Watching it gave her an odd sense of peace that what seemed an impossible situation was out of her hands to solve. With divine wisdom, the other members of Reliqui Fideles would get to the bottom of the machinations in the holy city. Soon she and Jacob would have a baby to love and care for, and that was her highest calling for the foreseeable future.

But where was Jacob? He should be back from his healing service at one of the markets by now. He'd planned to meet her in the nave, then sneak her into Matthias's study for a dinner discussion with Grandmother and Peter. Hopefully, all five of them would come to agreement about where Sarah and Jacob could hide safely for a short while.

She opened one of the bronze doors a crack. All was quiet in the entryway, so she crept down to Jacob's study, which she found empty and dark.

She rapped on Peter's open door. "Have you seen Jacob? He was supposed to meet me a while ago."

He looked up from his desk, where he'd been writing. "No. Maybe there's a long line at the Tower Gate." He shrugged. "I don't think Father's back yet either."

Her unease building, she debated returning to the nave or waiting in Jacob's study.

"You can have a seat." Peter waved her into the room. "The students and teachers are still at dinner, so it should be safe enough now."

But instead of sitting, Sarah stood in front of his window overlooking the shady courtyard. She reached for the teardrop necklace around her neck. Jacob should be back by now, and so should his father.

"What was that?" Peter asked a couple minutes later.

She turned from the window. "What?"

He seemed perplexed. "Didn't you say something?"

"No. Why?"

"That's so strange." He rubbed his forehead. "I thought I heard a woman say my name, like she was across a crowded room."

"I didn't hear anything," she said.

Peter rose from his desk. "That's the second time today." He put his hands in his pockets and paced across the room.

Sarah went back to staring out the window and worrying herself into a headache.

"Wait a minute." He came to an abrupt stop, then removed the silver Vasignis from his pocket. "I just heard it again, more clearly this time." He closed his eyes, tilting his head as if deep in thought. "And something about my father. That noise...it sounds like the square."

Her stomach lurched. "I have a bad feeling about this."

"Me too." Peter's bearded face was grim. "Come on. We have to get closer."

She followed him to a narrow window in the hallway overlooking the square.

"What do you see?" he asked.

Sarah stood on her tiptoes to peer between the veins of

lead. "Shoppers milling around the market. I think I see your father over by the candle maker's booth."

"Yes..." Peter's eyed were closed. "He's almost to the end of the row."

"He just passed the vegetable stand." She drew in a sharp breath as the high priest disappeared from her sight. "I can't see him anymore."

Several shoppers backed away from the busy booth, hands to their faces. Someone let out a high-pitched scream.

Peter's fingers squeezed the silver oval, his knuckles white. "I think he's on the ground. I see soldiers running."

Sarah squinted in the deepening twilight. "They're coming from the Tower Gate."

"He must be hurt." Peter leapt for the pull rope outside his study and rang for Caleb.

The clanging bells reverberated in her head, inducing nausea.

A minute later, Caleb appeared at the end of the hall, still chewing.

"Take me out to the square." Peter motioned for him to hurry. "We think Father's injured."

Sarah turned back to the window. A crowd had gathered in a circle. Soldiers burst through the periphery, several bending over someone. She gasped as they picked up the black-robed priest.

"They're carrying him to the door in the arcade. Remember, you're supposed to be blind," she called as Peter sped down the hallway, his lanky cousin a step behind.

Every single move mattered, and they needed any advantage they could get.

30

BELATED BLESSING

Sarah darted into Jacob's study and hid behind the thick folds of his heavy drapes. The jumbled noise of boots, armor, and swords obscured the frantic conversation between Peter and the soldiers carrying his father. But three terrible words cut through the approaching chaos—*knife, lung, and bleeding.*

As they stomped past her hiding place, she caught Peter's terse comment that they would all be better served if the soldiers would leave and apprehend his father's attacker, who was likely the same as his own.

A few minutes later, the clanking soldiers exited the door to the arcade. Sarah poked her head into the hallway while Peter shouted at Caleb for more cloths to staunch the bleeding. She grabbed every linen cloth in the alcove and raced to her father-in-law.

Groaning in agony, Matthias lay on his side on Peter's robe, with a wadded-up cloak for a pillow.

"Sarah, help me," Peter cried, his face nearly as ashen as his father's.

Matthias's bloody hand clawed at the knife in his back.

"Caleb, get to the Tower Gate. As soon as you see Jacob, tell him to hurry."

With one final horrified glance at the stricken high priest, he turned and ran.

"Remove this cursed blade from me." Vapors rose from the wound beneath his right shoulder blade.

"I know that smell." Peter's hand drifted to his scarred face. "That's the poison that burned me."

"Get it out." Matthias commanded through gritted teeth.

"We should wait for Jacob. He'll know what—"

"It burns me with unholy fire."

"The blade's poisoned and cursed," Sarah whispered as an image flashed in her mind of black tendrils wending their way through the high priest's body.

"All right..." Peter's fearful eyes found hers.

She laid a hand on his father's shoulder, willing the Sacred Fire within her to join his in battle.

With one swift tug, Peter removed the steaming dagger and flung it to the floor.

As Matthias's breathing slowed, he clutched the front of his son's robe. "The final—"

"No, Jacob's coming."

"This mortal body is beyond saving, even for Jacob." A sputtering cough racked his chest, and he grimaced in pain.

"No." Peter bent over him. "I—I'm not ready, Father."

Matthias reached a trembling hand to his temple. "You have been given eyes to see through the darkness. You will be made ready."

Tears slipped from Peter's sightless eyes as he gripped his father's arm, willing him to wait for Jacob.

"Sarah..." The high priest turned his head, bloody spittle running down his gray beard.

"Yes, Father." She reached for his hand.

"I'm sorry." His chest rattled as he drew in a breath. "Tell Jacob I give you my blessing."

"I will."

"I wish I could hold the baby...the Heir."

"I know, Father." Sarah took his other hand from the pool of blood spreading beneath him, and placed it on her abdomen. "Meet your grandson."

His brown eyes fluttered closed, a hint of a smile on his blue-tinged lips as the baby kicked.

"Peter..." he whispered, the rattle in his chest worsening. "The final anointing."

His face constricted with grief, Peter removed a small vial from his trouser pocket. Taking a deep breath, he uncorked the oil and rested his fingertips on the center of his father's forehead.

"May the loving hand of the living God be upon you in your hour of suffering, Father." He forced down a sob. "And may the Sacred Fire that burns within you light your way home."

They stared in silence as his breathing slowed. Then High Priest Matthias's chest rose with a final shuddering breath. His face slackened as his worldly cares slipped away.

Sarah gently placed his bloody hand by his side. A single shining drop of blood hung from his wrist. Time seemed to slow as she watched the prophesied drop pull away and fall to the floor, spattering at her feet. "Go in peace, Father."

"No, this can't be," Peter whispered. Tears trickled down his cheeks as he bowed his head in silent prayer.

Sarah lightly touched his shoulder, offering a tiny gift of peace to the next High Priest of Aclesia as he bid goodbye to the current one.

Bells jangled down the hall, jarring them from their shock and grief.

"Jacob's coming," Caleb called. "He's through the gate." The teen gave a whimpering cry when he saw they were too late.

"Peter! Caleb!" Jacob's footsteps pounded toward them. "What happened?"

Steeling herself, Sarah turned to face her distraught husband.

His eyes widened at the sight of her bloody dress. "The baby? No!" He clasped his head in his hands.

She rushed to him. "We're all right. It's your father."

He looked from Sarah to Peter, who stared numbly at their father's lifeless body on his desk.

"What?"

"He's dead." Peter said flatly. "Stabbed in the square."

Sarah took Jacob by the arm as he stumbled to his father's side.

Matthias's face seemed peaceful in death, more so than life.

Shouts rang out in the main hallway of the school. "What's going on?" boomed the voice of Brother Augustus.

"There's a huge crowd gathered in the square," someone else called.

Peter roused himself from his stupor. "Caleb, go with Sarah to the tunnel, and bring back holy water."

Their cousin wiped his blotchy face with the back of his sleeve. "Yes..."

Jacob turned to Sarah. "Get back to the bakery and stay there. I'll come as soon as I can."

Seated at the kitchen table in a clean dress, Sarah stared at her dinner of leftovers.

"You'd better eat something." Marta twisted her dishtowel. "You'll need your strength for the days ahead. We all will."

But what would the days ahead bring? More bloodshed? Sarah couldn't even bring herself to pick up her fork.

George sat across from her, periodically rubbing his hand over his bald head.

The front door opened, and he was on his feet, club raised.

"Sarah?" Grandmother called.

"In the kitchen." He lowered his club.

"We heard Matthias was stabbed. It must have been right after leaving our council meeting. There's a vigil in the square." Grandmother flew into the kitchen, breathless. "People are trying to get through the gate, but the soldiers aren't letting anyone in. They're even questioning everyone leaving the Heights."

Sarah rose from the table. "Matthias is dead."

"No..." She braced herself on the counter. "How could that happen in such a public area?"

"It was getting dark. He was almost back to the cathedral when he was assaulted. Peter thinks it was the same woman who attacked him."

"It's too dangerous for you here." Grandmother spun around. "Marta, pack her things."

"I can't leave without Jacob," she said. "And where would we even go?"

"You could reach Havilah tonight. George, hurry to the stables and hire a carriage."

He shook his head. "The north gate will be closed before we can get there, and we need to think this through."

Grandmother's hazel eyes darted to Sarah's midsection. "You're carrying the baby low now. We have very little time to think things through."

31

FELLOWSHIP FRAYING

"I should be at Matthias's funeral," Sarah insisted the next morning.

"No, you shouldn't." Grandmother paced the kitchen, too agitated to sit. "Not under these circumstances."

"It's too dangerous," Jacob agreed. "The fortunetellers might try to draw you out again."

Marta set a cup of tea on the counter for Grandmother, but she ignored it.

"Sylvaneus started the council meeting late, and he seemed reluctant to let it end. Had the meeting ended on time, your father would have walked home in daylight."

"I was delayed too," Jacob raked his hand through his dark bangs. "Some man kept insisting I heal his injured knee. I prayed for him, but it was obvious he had no faith. I don't even think he was hurt. Then when I was leaving the market, a woman ran into me and fell. Of course, I had to make sure she was all right."

"Whoever our enemies may be, they are cunning and ruthless," Grandmother said.

"What have the guards found so far?" Sarah asked.

"Peter and I had a tense conversation with Commander Xavier this morning. He suggested they had some promising leads, but he wouldn't provide details no matter how many times we asked. So we don't believe they're making much progress in finding Father's killer."

Sarah stared at the untouched bread on the table in front of her. "Maybe Demetrius knows more."

"Yes, and I hope he'll send a message to us," Grandmother said. "But the sooner we get you to one of our safe houses, the better. We can leave for Havilah this afternoon. George and I can take you, then—

"Wait a minute." Jacob rose from the table. "I can't leave before my father's funeral. I have to be there to help consecrate Peter as the next high priest and lay my father to rest."

"Yes, but the funeral's not for two days." Grandmother planted her hands on her hips. "Sarah could be safely hidden by then, and I can be back for the funeral too."

"I have to protect her." His panicked eyes darted to Sarah's belly. "She and the baby aren't completely safe unless she's with me."

"What makes you think you can stop an assassin that's always a couple steps ahead of us? Especially when you couldn't even heal your own brother."

Jacob rounded on her. "I'm her husband. You're just her grandmother. What makes you think you get to make these decisions?"

"I'm right here, and I can speak for myself." Sarah stood. "I love you both, but this arguing is getting us nowhere...and giving me a headache."

"You're right. I'm sorry." Jacob ran his palm down his stricken face.

Sarah held out her hands. "We need to trust each other, especially at a time like this."

"Ever the peacemaker," Marta said from the sink.

"I'm sorry too." Grandmother shook her head. "You've just lost your father, Jacob. I had no call to lose my temper."

He turned toward the window. "I didn't even get to say goodbye."

Sarah slipped her hand into his. "But he did…by giving us his blessing. That's how he said goodbye."

He squeezed her hand. "I can't lose you too."

"We can all agree on that." Grandmother brought her tea to the kitchen table. "Now what do you both want to do?"

"Sarah and I should leave together right after my father's funeral, but I'm not sure where we should go."

"The Fourth Scroll said there was a hidden host." Sarah lowered herself onto a chair across from her grandmother. "What does that mean?"

"I don't know," Jacob sat next to her. "Does Reliqui Fideles have a mysterious group stationed outside of the city that I'm not aware of?"

Grandmother pursed her lips. "I wish that were the case. We just have a handful of safe houses within a day or two of here that we use to help freed slaves get back home."

He propped his elbows on the table. "Maybe there's a hidden remnant somewhere, a few families that never left a remote valley after Kadmiel was defeated. Some were found centuries later, but a couple thousand years? That doesn't seem possible."

"No, and we need an immediate solution." Grandmother reached for her tea. "In a larger city like Bethuliah, Sarah can blend in, but you're too easily recognized."

"Wait," Sarah said. "What about the orphanage, with Elena and Amos? It's well hidden and only a half day's ride from here."

"Yes, that could work." Grandmother set down her empty cup. "And Elena is a capable midwife. But how would you explain your absence, Jacob?"

"The mourning period lasts for seven days after the funeral. Peter can make up a story about me needing time to myself to grieve, that I blame myself for not returning in time to save father." He looked down at the table. "At least there's some truth to that."

"His death was in no way your fault." Sarah's heart ached for her husband who would carry yet another undeserved wound.

"Delegations will start arriving soon after that from the closer cities," Grandmother said, "and you need to be home to receive them."

"I know. In the meantime, Brother Augustus can help cover for me, but there shouldn't be many people in the cathedral. Peter is sending the students home for their own safety. I doubt any will return until Father's killer has been caught. Maybe not even then."

Sarah rested her hand on her tight belly. "I sure hope the baby doesn't take another whole week to be born."

"I just pray he doesn't come in the next two days." Grandmother said. "I'll send word for Jonah to come with Seth and Marilla to the funeral. Then Sarah can leave the city with them and the rest of the crowd right after the funeral. I'll come first thing the next morning, and Seth can take us to the orphanage."

"Look, I've accepted that Jonah's my brother-in-law, but I'm not about to trust the wellbeing of my wife and child to him." Jacob crossed his arms over his chest. "I'll leave for Havilah right after my father's laid to rest."

"But how will you get there?" Sarah asked.

"There's a hole in the eastern wall behind the cemetery. I'll climb down to the road and walk to Havilah if I have to."

"That's so steep. Are you sure you can manage in the dark?"

He gave a wry smile. "We've smuggled others out in the dark. Why not myself?"

"I'll have Goran wait for you outside the city with his carriage, then take you to Havilah," Grandmother said. "It's crucial that you not be seen in public when you should be observing the mourning period with Peter."

"I know."

"Then is this plan agreeable?"

Sarah nodded. "We don't seem to have any better alternatives."

Jacob turned to her. "Promise you won't leave Havilah without me."

She leaned over and kissed his cheek. "I promise."

HANNAH WASN'T the only one whose bloodshot eyes were drawn to the empty seat across the table from her. Many of her fellow councilors stared numbly where Matthias had sat yesterday afternoon. Today there were no side conversations or bartering for support for some policy or project.

The ornate double doors to the chamber opened. Sylvaneus lumbered in, his bulbous face downcast in a vain attempt to mimic the grief and horror of most of the councilors assembled.

"It is with great sadness and distress that I call this emergency meeting to order, our second in as many days." Sylvaneus surveyed the packed room. "But we must remain resolute in our duties, to honor the memory of our dear friend and colleague, Father Matthias."

Hannah fought the urge to call out such a stunning display of hypocrisy.

Sylvaneus nodded to his right. "I believe Commander Xavier has an update to share."

She narrowed her eyes. Why was the high priest's seat empty? "Where is Peter? Did you not think to invite him?"

"He's not the high priest yet." Niccolus waved his hand. "Not until tomorrow at sundown if I understand the archaic practice correctly."

"Indeed." Sylvaneus huffed at the interruption. "Commander Xavier, please proceed."

"But it's only appropriate for him to be here," Councilor Miranda cut in. "Especially since both attacks were likely the work of the same person. And clearly his father was the intended target the first time too."

"If so, we should know shortly." The commander puffed out his chest. "I'm pleased to announce that within the past hour we took a suspect into custody."

Gasps echoed throughout the chamber.

"Witnesses placed her at the scene?" Sebastian asked.

"We have his confession."

Hannah did a double take. "His? Isn't the attacker a woman?"

"No, in this case the attacker is a man," Xavier said, "although we have good reason to believe the two events are connected."

"Well, who is he?" Miranda demanded when the room fell silent. "And why target the high priest?"

"A petty criminal addicted to street spice." The commander crossed his arms. "A mere pawn in a larger scheme."

"What scheme?" several councilors asked at once.

"We're still unraveling this tangled web, but there are surely accomplices." The commander's hand curled into a fist. "With persuasive questioning, we believe he'll divulge the identity of the man who hired him."

"But how can you be certain the culprit is a man?" Hannah asked.

"It would be premature to say, but we believe the person behind this murderous plot was close to the high priest. Close enough to know his movements, and that he would attend our emergency meeting last evening."

Close to him? It couldn't possibly be a fellow priest, could it? Matthias could be difficult and a bit gruff at times, but what would motivate one of his own to betray him? A large sum of money? Hannah narrowed her eyes. Or perhaps Xavier, or someone else in this chamber, was spinning his own tangled web of deceit.

The commander rested his forearms on the table. "Clearly, this person is extraordinarily dangerous and seems intent on sending a message."

Hannah would bet that whatever message Xavier thinks the murderer is sending won't reflect well on the priesthood.

She scanned the perimeter of the room that held at least thirty people. "Of course, everyone here knew about our meeting, including many of their family members and associates."

Sylvaneus cleared his throat. "And that is why we can divulge no further details at this time."

32

———

DRINK FROM THIS CUP

Jacob gripped the silver chalice of Eleazar, careful not to slosh wine on his robe. Behind him, Brother Augustus and five more priests lifted his father's casket, the purple and white vestment of the high priest draped over the top.

"Are you ready?" he whispered to Peter.

"I'd better be." Peter tightened his hold on the silver scepter.

During the private funeral service that afternoon, Augustus had reminded all the priests of their vow to uphold the Priestly Codex and present unified support for Peter, which was especially important given his young age. What went unmentioned was his impaired eyesight. Jacob suspected doubts about his brother's ability to assume the role of high priest lingered, both inside and outside the House of Eleazar.

The black-robed choir behind them began their low funeral dirge.

Peter grasped Jacob's forearm for him to guide him to the square. "When we get to the bottom of the steps, I'm going to let go of you."

"What?" Jacob turned to his brother as the cathedral's huge double doors opened.

"Our enemies want me to look weak, but now is not the time for weakness."

"No, it's not," Jacob whispered despite the crushing weight of all their enemies had wrought, and the impending flight from the holy city for both him and Sarah, a plan that left him with growing unease.

He led Peter down the steps, not that he needed help since he had the Vasignis in his pocket and flaming scepter in his other hand. "Just keep pretending you're blind. We don't want our enemies to think otherwise."

At the bottom, Peter let go of him. "Without the Sacred Fire, I am blind."

Jacob dropped a half step behind his brother, who was soon to become Father Peter. Only twelve years ago, the two of them had stood in this same spot for the consecration of their father, after the passing of their grandfather. Twelve years seemed like such a short time compared to most of the high priests who had come before.

Had Father suspected that the vision of Obadiah presaged a bloody and premature end to his life? If so, he opened the Fourth Scroll anyway, setting in motion events they couldn't control and a future they could only guess at.

A smattering of sobs and sniffles accompanied the six priests as they processed down the wide stone steps. They lowered their father's casket onto a stand draped in flowing purple cloth.

Peter leaned over. "Not such a great turnout for Father."

"Not unless you count all the soldiers." Jacob squinted into the setting sun.

Only residents of the Heights and free citizens with the most stringent clearance were allowed into the square. Yet guards in full armor patrolled the top of the wall and ringed the perimeter. Did they think the killer was here, poised to attack again? Were fortunetellers hiding in the crowd whispering curses? The sooner he and Peter got back inside to deliver their father's body to the crypts, the better.

"Look at those pompous fools pretending to grieve," Peter whispered.

The councilors and their family members sat in several rows of chairs placed to their left. Sylvaneus had the political wisdom to look grief stricken for those gathered in the square. A few seats down, Niccolus sat with his dour wife whom he'd long ago abandoned for mistresses. Apparently, he had other plans for the evening as he kept checking his pocket watch. Hannah sat alone on the end, her cheeks sunken and pale.

It wasn't until Peter began to deliver the invocation that Jacob realized the choir had finished their dirge. The choir, teaching priests, and remaining students stood silently behind the casket.

He straightened his shoulders and folded his hands in front of him, trying to look like he was listening to his brother. With his full beard and commanding presence, Peter bore a strong resemblance to the portrait of their father with their late mother at twenty-five years of age.

Now parentless and about to become a father himself, the grief Jacob had forced down for the last several days threatened to bubble to the surface. He stole another glance at Hannah. Was she also setting aside her grief until he and Sarah were safely away, so she could give birth to the last high priest?

Brother Augustus gave him a subtle nudge. He looked down at the silver chalice of Eleazar in his hands, then took a couple jerky steps to stand before Peter.

Jacob cleared his burning throat. "Do you Peter, son of Matthias, son of Mordecai, willingly take this cup of the holy covenant between the living God and the House of Eleazar?"

"I do." Peter took the chalice from him. "I, Peter, priest of the House of Eleazar, drink from this cup like my fathers before me, pledging my service as high priest until my death or the coming of the Heir to the Sacred Fire." He brought the silver cup to his lips and drank of the red wine.

Jacob took the empty chalice back from his brother. "May the living God pour out his spirit upon you, Father Peter."

Brother Augustus stepped forward and removed the high priest's vestment from atop the casket. Peter dipped his head as the old priest placed the purple garment around his neck.

"Brothers and sisters in the faith..." Peter's voice rang out across the square. "Here at the advent of my appointed time as high priest, I stand before you broken and scarred. Though I have not earthly sight, I have the blood of Eleazar in my veins and the Sacred Fire in my heart."

Cheers arose from the other side of the wall, accompanied by a few polite claps from the audience in the square.

"I know the days ahead will not be easy, so I ask you to stand with me, praying for peace for the holy city, and for our beloved cathedral. I am not blind to the challenges we face, for there have always been those who would oppose us and our faith." He turned his head toward the council, the Arcanus family at the forefront. "But the living God will see us through these days of darkness and grief."

Niccolus and several of his allies sneered.

"And when they have passed, new blessings will spring forth." Peter lifted the silver scepter high. "For the promises of Patrimus will stand, and his purposes will be fulfilled, now and in the age to come."

"May it be so!" A voice called from the other side of the wall. *May it be so* echoed throughout the square and beyond.

"May it be so," Jacob whispered, for the promised Heir was coming very soon.

SEATED near the window in the parlor, Sarah listened to the faint notes of the funeral dirge. Not only did she mourn the loss of Matthias, but at the conclusion of his funeral and Peter's consecration, her life in this house for the past two years would come to an end. Maybe, when it was safe to return to the holy city with her husband and baby, their next chapter would be even better. But seeing as her son was the Heir to the Sacred Fire, life would never be the same.

Jonah sat across from her on the sofa, polishing his sword.

She scowled. "I'm not sure why you decided to bring that."

He shrugged. "Just in case we have any trouble on the way."

"We'll be in a carriage the entire time, but I suppose if you cut yourself, Jacob can heal you when he gets to Havilah."

Marta brought her another cup of tea, as if she consumed the beverage at the same rapid rate as Grandmother. Or maybe the poor woman was just trying to keep busy in the midst of their grief and upheaval.

"Thank you, Marta."

She patted Sarah's arm. "You're welcome, dear."

"I just wish I could be there with Jacob. This must be so hard for him and Peter."

Jonah sheathed his sword. "I thought the high priest was mean and didn't think you were good enough for Jacob."

Sarah looked down at her hand that had clasped Matthias's in his final moments. "I think he had a change of heart about me in the end."

"Not sure why it took him so long," Marta said.

Someone banged on the front door.

Sarah and Marta stilled, but Jonah rushed to the window and peeked through the curtain. "It looks like a girl. She's running away."

"Stay here," George called from the hallway. "I'll see what this is about."

Marta patted her chest. "Maybe she has the wrong house."

George returned to the parlor, a small envelope in hand. "It's addressed to S. E."

"Apparently, not the wrong house," Jonah said as Sarah rose from her chair.

George handed her the envelope with a black wax seal and the letters R.F. inside a symbol of a flame.

"Demetrius..." Marta sucked in her breath. "This can't be good."

"Open it." Jonah moved closer.

Sarah broke the seal and pulled out a folded paper.

Her mouth fell open. "That can't be right."

Jonah jostled her. "What does it say?"

She blinked and read the message a second time, then a third.

"What is it?" Marta whispered.

Her hand trembled. "Under orders to arrest Jacob as accessory to murder."

Jonah reached for the hilt of his sword. "Jacob killed someone?"

"No, of course not." Sarah sank into the chair by the fireplace. "The guards must think he had his father killed."

"And his brother blinded." George ran a huge hand over his head. "He's been set up."

"Heaven help us." Marta fanned herself.

"Wait. Who's Demetrius?" Jonah asked.

"Our father's friend who kept that sword for you all these years. And a captain of the guard." Sarah handed the note to George.

"That looks like Demetrius's scrawl." He tossed the evidence in the fireplace.

"Can we trust him?" Jonah asked as they watched the horrifying message burn.

Marta wrung her hands. "If we can't trust Demetrius, we can't trust anybody."

Sarah pushed herself up from the chair. "We've got to warn Jacob."

"How?" Jonah asked. "You can't just barge into that funeral."

"What if they plan to arrest him soon?" She turned to George, her panic rising. "Didn't you say there were lots of soldiers on the wall and at the gate?"

His shoulders tensed. "Demetrius wouldn't have risked sending that message if it wasn't urgent."

"Whoever's behind this must know the Fourth Scroll has been opened." Sarah's jaw clenched. "They don't want to weaken the House of Eleazar—they want to destroy it."

"Oh, my word." Marta turned to her husband.

George's eyes darted to the window. "But who's pulling the strings? The fortunetellers or the House of Arcanus?"

With a burst of anger, Sarah turned to Jonah. "An Arcanus murdered our parents and cursed us. I won't let them take my husband and leave my son fatherless."

"But how can we get to Jacob?"

"They're going to lay Matthias to rest in the crypts after the ceremony. We have to get there first."

"What about the plan?" George's brow creased. "You need to leave for Havilah with Seth and Marilla, otherwise the gates will be closed for the night."

"I'm not leaving without Jacob." Her voice broke. "Otherwise, I might never see him again."

Five minutes later, the four of them entered the basement storeroom. Sarah clutched a burlap bag with her possessions. Jonah's hand hovered over the pommel of his sword.

"Tell Grandmother not to worry," Sarah said. "We'll see her in Havilah in the morning."

Marta pulled her into a hug. "The poor woman will be in for a sleepless night. We all will."

George lifted the tapestry concealing the entrance of the tunnel to the cathedral. "I'll have Seth and Marilla wait for you outside the north gate, where the road forks for Havilah." His forehead crinkled with worry. "You'll have a bit of a walk to get there."

"I know." Sarah stood on her tip toes to kiss his cheek. "Thank you, George."

He handed her his candle. "May the living God watch over you both."

Jonah scurried into the tunnel after Sarah. "I don't have fond memories of this."

"Jacob saved you from being arrested when you were drunk and stupid. Now he needs our help."

"Just don't let that candle go out."

"I won't." Sarah cupped her hand around the flame.

"Let me hold it."

"No, you need to be quiet."

Not only had Jonah inherited their grandmother's hazel eyes but also her intense dislike of confined spaces.

As they crept into the cavern beneath the cathedral, Sarah heard the sound of low chanting. Torches flickered at the base of the wide stone staircase, and the Sacred Fire burned at the arched entrance to the crypts.

The chanting grew louder as they hurried toward the underground stream.

Jonah swallowed hard. "There're dead bodies over there?"

"Yes, and there's about to be one more." Sarah blew out her candle. "We've got to get out of sight."

They entered the mouth of the tunnel the stream had carved over millennia.

He groaned. "What is it about priests and tunnels?"

"Hush," Sarah whispered as her brother clung to her arm like a small child.

IN SOLEMN SILENCE, the Brothers filed out of the crypts ahead of Jacob and Peter. Despite the profound finality of laying their father to rest with the high priests of centuries past, no tears would come for Jacob.

Peter turned to leave. "You coming?"

"Yes." He needed to eat dinner and speak with Augustus before sneaking out of the cathedral under the cover of darkness. At least Sarah would be on her way to Havilah by now.

As they passed the Sacred Fire guarding the entrance to the crypts, Jacob stumbled to a stop. "I thought I just heard a woman whisper my name."

"Oh, great." Peter glanced at the white flame. "Now you're hearing things too."

"My mind must be playing tricks on me," he said as they crossed the narrow stone bridge. "Wait, I just heard it again."

Peter's brow furrowed. "A fortuneteller?"

"No, it sounded like—"

Jacob spun to his left.

"Sarah?" He bounded past the cistern to her. "What are you doing here? You're supposed to be leaving now."

"I know, but we need to go together, as soon as possible."

"Why? What happened?"

"And why is he here?" Peter demanded as Jonah stepped out of the shadows, a sword strapped to his belt.

"The soldiers are coming to arrest you." Sarah grasped the sleeve of Jacob's robe. "They think you hired someone to murder your father."

"What?" He couldn't seem to make sense of her breathless words.

"We got a message from Demetrius. They're supposed to arrest you as an accessory to murder."

Peter turned to him in horror. "You've been framed."

Jacob's head swam. "No, this has to be a terrible mistake."

"Of course..." Peter pointed at his chest. "You couldn't heal my blindness, you didn't save that soldier at the Anointing, and you didn't get to Father in time."

"Those two were already dead."

"I know, but just think how this looks. And there's already bad blood between us and the city guard. It wouldn't take much planted evidence for them to believe the allegation."

"The fortunetellers have to be behind this," Sarah said.

"And they must have friends in high places to pull this off." Peter stroked his beard. "Like the Arcanus clan."

An image flashed in Jacob's mind of the many soldiers in full armor in the square...and Niccolus Arcanus checking his watch.

"We don't have time for this." Sarah's green eyes pleaded with him to move.

"She's right. You have to go now," Peter said.

"But I'm innocent."

"You'll never get a fair trial with Niccolus Arcanus as the Chief Magistrate," Peter said. "He'd rather see you hang."

"They'll kill you too."

"No, I've heard how they speak of me...a blind fool who will drive the cathedral and school into ruin." He shook his head with a rueful laugh. "They're counting on me to finish off the House of Eleazar."

"Jacob, they could come for you any minute." Sarah clasped his hand, trying to pull him toward the mouth of the tunnel.

Peter headed for the wide stone staircase. "I'll get the key to the gate, otherwise you won't get very far."

Jacob took a deep breath. "Get my bag from our sitting room too."

Sarah hurried them into the mouth of the tunnel and explained how they would meet up with Seth on the road to Havilah.

He leaned against the cold stone wall. "I can't believe anyone thinks I'm responsible for my father's murder."

"I know, but the truth will come out." She squeezed his hand. "Grandmother and Peter will fight for you, and Reliqui Fideles will get to the bottom of this horrible scheme. It's just a matter of time."

"Could the fortunetellers have figured out I'm the father of the Heir? Did I give it away when I was looking around for you at the Anointing?"

"I don't know, but it doesn't matter now," she said.

Five agonizing minutes later, Peter hurried down the stairs, a keyring in his hand. He grabbed a torch from a sconce.

"I'll stall them as long as I can." He handed the torch to Jonah and the keyring to Jacob.

"Watch your back." Jacob embraced his brother. "The holy city needs a high priest, especially now."

"It needs the Heir to the Sacred Fire even more." Peter kissed Sarah on the cheek.

He extended his hand to Jonah. "Don't do anything stupid."

For the next half hour, they followed the narrow path beside the underground stream. Jacob's mind raced trying to decipher who could have orchestrated this diabolical conspiracy. Niccolus Arcanus had never struck him as that smart. But who else could be the linchpin? Maybe the mysterious Seer?

"At least this route is all downhill." Sarah broke the silence.

"Yeah, but it's starting to smell worse." Jonah covered his nose with his sleeve.

Jacob looked over his shoulder. "The sewage means we've got about five minutes to go."

From the rear, Jonah let out a disgusted groan.

More fearful thoughts plagued Jacob. Would Sarah have the stamina to trek another hour to reach the carriage? Would the coming darkness conceal them or put them at greater risk?

He dunked the flaming end of his torch in the stream with a loud hiss.

"What are you doing?" Jonah cried.

"Look."

The last rays of daylight shone through a thick iron gate about twenty feet ahead.

"Fresh air, at last." Sarah inhaled deeply.

Jacob removed the keyring from the pocket of his robe. "Jonah, help me with the gate."

He clambered past Sarah on the narrow ledge, his foot slipping into the stream with a loud splash. "Now my boot's all wet!"

Jacob turned the key in the rusty lock. "Just push."

The heavy gate creaked open, and they hurried onto a sandy path along the boulder strewn river bank.

"There's no going back now." He glanced at Sarah, then tossed the keyring far into the tunnel.

Behind her, a woman stepped out of the shadows.

33

UP RIVER

With a startled yelp, Jonah drew his sword. Jacob leapt toward Sarah.

Straight black hair framed the woman's unconcerned face.

"Fiona?" Sarah waved her brother off. "Put that away. She's part of Reliqui Fideles."

"What are you doing out here?" Jacob whispered.

Jonah sheathed his sword. "You were the one who delivered that note to Sarah."

"Yes." She looked up at the high wall, but no guards were visible. "Demetrius sent me. We figured this was your best way out of the city."

"Why do the guards think I killed my father?" Jacob asked.

Fiona walked up the sandy path, motioning for them to keep as close to the wall as possible. "They have a man in custody who claims you hired him."

"Then the man's a liar," Jacob hissed.

"And he's addicted to street spice, which probably made him desperate enough to do someone's bidding to frame you. Demetrius said Commander Xavier wants to make an example of you since he looked like a fool after chaos broke out at the Anointing. And the council's pressuring him to make an arrest for your father's murder."

"I bet I can guess who's pushing him the most."

"The House of Arcanus?" Sarah said.

"Of course." Fiona nodded as they picked their way through the encroaching darkness to an old dock jutting into the river.

She held out her hand to Jacob. "Give me your robe."

He slipped it off. "Why?"

"Because they will know soon enough that you've fled the city, and we might as well let them think you went south." She wadded up the robe and handed it to Jonah. "Drop that in the bottom of that small rowboat in the weeds, and push it into the river."

"You have to stay off the road until you get at least a quarter mile from the city," Fiona said as Jonah attended to his task. "Soldiers are patrolling outside the city and will question any priests going back to their villages in case they're accomplices of yours."

"Accomplices? This is madness." Jacob watched the black wad float away as Jonah climbed back up to the path.

"No, it's intimidation." Fiona scowled. "And planting the idea in their minds that you're guilty of a despicable crime."

"But how can we get to Havilah?" Sarah asked. "Seth is waiting for us near the north gate with a carriage, and Grandmother's supposed to meet us there tomorrow morning."

Fiona's eyes widened at the sound of hoofbeats in the distance. "You can't go anywhere near the north gate."

Jacob shook his head. "But we can't stay here, and Sarah's in no condition to trek through the woods."

"There's another rowboat tied up under the dock." Jonah pointed. "It looks big enough to hold us, and there's not much current now."

They inspected the boat, which was in better shape than the one that bore Jacob's robe down river.

"As long as we stay near the shore, we should be good." Jonah worked on untying the rope. "We can get past the patrols then come ashore."

"Do we even have any food and water?" Jacob asked.

Sarah held up her burlap bag. "I have a loaf of bread Marta insisted we bring."

"There's a rock formation that looks like a crouching lion on the High Plain of Nirel," Fiona said. "Under the right front paw, there's a stash of food and supplies to start a fire. It makes a good shelter for the night."

"I remember that place from when I first came to the city." Sarah also recalled the steep hill to reach it.

Jacob squinted in the growing darkness. "That's still a long way off."

"I'll rest in the boat, and we don't have a better alternative."

"I'll get word to your grandmother to meet you there in the morning instead of going to Havilah," Fiona said.

A few minutes later, Sarah eased herself down on the hard seat. While it felt good to get off her swollen feet, she doubted the feeling would last long. Jacob sat in front, his oar resting on his knees.

Jonah gave them a firm shove into the murky river and hopped in the back of the boat. Sarah waved to Fiona as she used a tree branch like a broom to sweep away their tracks.

Only twice in the next half hour did they hear a patrol on the river road, but they ducked down below the reeds and scrub that lined the shore. The sporadic traffic mostly came from carriages or riders on horseback.

As the lights of the city retreated in the distance, Sarah's thoughts turned to the baby kicking in her belly. How strange that both his parents would be forced to flee the holy city. Wherever they ended up in their temporary exile, she hoped it would be a place of peace. They had endured enough violence and heartache.

Her eyelids fluttered closed with the rhythmic sound of the oars cutting through the water, and Jacob and Jonah's labored breathing. She prayed for protection for those left behind, Grandmother, Peter, Marta, and—

"What is that?" Jonah's oar dragged in the water, and the boat drifted.

Sarah's eyes snapped open. As she stared at the orange glow on the horizon, a shudder passed through her. The sun had set almost an hour ago, and now it appeared ready to rise again. "Kadmiel's canyon…"

A low howl sounded in the distance, and yellow sparks wafted skyward. As a dry wind blew the loose strands of hair off Sarah's face, her head began to throb.

Jacob plunged his oar into the river. "Row harder."

Something soft and gray landed on Sarah's hand. She swiped at it, leaving a streak of ash. Soon ash dotted Jacob's back as he bent forward to pull them through the water.

The wind grew hotter, buffeting them with the stench of decay and death.

"That smells worse than the tunnel," Jonah cried.

Lightning flashed, illuminating the jagged rocks of Kadmiel's canyon, that hideous monument of evil on the barren plains. Sarah's stomach lurched as the canyon belched glowing embers into the night. But it wasn't the canyon assailing them. It was the hate-filled spirit that inhabited it, cursing them on Ventus Furens…the raging wind.

She threw her arm over her nose and mouth as the choking smoke and ash thickened. Borne on the howling wind were three words she never wanted to hear again. *You will pay.*

Orange embers hissed as they fell to the water.

"We have to get off the river!" Jacob shouted over his shoulder.

A glowing coal landed on Jonah's pant leg, and a tiny flame leapt up, feeding on the cloth and the wind.

"Jonah, your leg." She dipped her hand in the river and flung water at him.

"Ah!" The boat rocked when he stood, slapping at his pants. His oar slipped into the water as another ember grazed his face. He twisted away, then plunged over the side into the dark current.

"Jonah!" Sarah gripped the sides of the boat as it spun.

He emerged a few moments later in waist high water, his wet face tinged orange in the eerie dusk. As the boat drifted away from him with the current, Jacob threw him the rope.

"Pull us to shore!"

He dragged the boat until it scraped bottom then collapsed on a rocky strip by a few battered shrubs.

Jacob hurled their bags onto the bank then stepped into the shallow water and carried Sarah to dry land.

She doubled over coughing as smoke and ash drifted past.

"Come on. We need to find shelter." Jacob helped her toward the road. "Bring our bags, Jonah."

He got to his feet. "I'm not sure why I should take orders from you."

On the far side of the rutted road, they found a clearing behind several large boulders. Jonah dropped her burlap bag and Jacob's satchel next to Sarah as she leaned against a tree to catch her breath. Above the hazy smoke, the silhouette of the mountain lion outcropping was visible in the moonlight.

She pointed her shaking hand at the edge of the High Plain of Nirel. "That's where Fiona said we'd find food and shelter."

"But you're in no condition to trek up that hill," Jacob said.

"It's more like a small mountain." Jonah shivered in his wet clothes.

At the moment, she couldn't disagree. But maybe once she recovered from the firestorm...

"My sword." Jonah spun around. "It's still in the boat."

"Leave it for now," Sarah urged.

"No, I might need it." He raced back toward the river.

Leaves rustled as the sulfurous wind picked up again. Only Jonah would be foolish enough to run toward the darkest of all spirits.

Jacob peered into the forest. "I can see a light in there."

Faint firelight flickered through the swaying branches.

"What do you think it is? A farm or small village?" Sarah thought they would've been past the outlying villages by now.

"I don't know, but it's going to get cold tonight." Jacob ran his hands up and down the arms of his thin coat. "Maybe there's an inn, or a barn, at least."

Strangely, Sarah wasn't cold. Her necklace warmed her chest, almost uncomfortably so.

Jacob snaked his way into the trees. "I'm going to take a closer look."

"Don't be long." She reached her hand inside her cloak. The teardrop amulet burned hot on her skin.

She pulled her hand back just before a thick arm clamped across her chest. Even worse was the blade pressed to her throat.

34

NOTHING OF WORTH

Jacob whipped around at the sound of Sarah's startled cry. He crashed through the underbrush and stumbled to a stop in the clearing where a heavy-set bearded man held a knife to his wife's throat. A balding man stood next to them, a large club in his hand.

"Let her go." Jacob forced the words from his dry mouth.

Sarah's eyes locked on his, then she turned her head slightly to her captor. "The two of us mean you no harm."

The bearded man laughed. "I'd not be worried if either of you did."

Two. Jacob gave her a barely perceptible nod. The men didn't know about Jonah, wherever he happened to be. And thankfully, Jonah hadn't brought any personal belongings, aside from his precious sword.

Jacob gestured to their two bags at the base of a jagged rock and said loudly, "Take what you want, and we'll be on our way."

"Oh, we will." The balding man snatched their bags from the ground. "After we get to our camp. Now move." He pointed with his club to a break in the trees about ten yards away. "Hands on your heads."

His heart thudding in his chest, Jacob entered what seemed to be a deer path. He could barely see in front of him and held out his hand to push the low hanging branches out of the way. For that he received a sharp jab to his lower back.

Sarah gasped behind him.

"Our family is expecting us," she said, a slight tremor in her voice.

"That's what they all say." The big man brought up the rear.

"They'll come and search for us." Jacob prayed his brother-in-law was in hearing distance.

"By the time they do, we'll be long gone."

A light shone about twenty yards ahead. The path widened into a clearing bordered by boulders and thick evergreens. A small fire burned in the center. A grimy frying pan and cook pot sat in the dirt near a pile of clothing and supplies. An older man was packing the spoils of their thievery into the saddle bags of a speckled gray mare.

"See, I told you I heard voices on the river road." Still clutching Sarah, the bearded man waved his knife.

The old man scrunched his weathered face. "You got a pregnant woman."

The bearded bandit lowered his knife and backed away in surprise. "Well, I'll be."

Sarah rubbed her throat, a red welt visible in the firelight.

"Sit down, miss, before you drop that baby at my feet." He gestured toward a fallen tree a few feet away from the fire.

Jacob leaned over to help her, and the balding man clubbed him in the knee. He toppled over. When he tried to rise, the man shoved him down on the log next to Sarah and tied his hands behind him.

"Let's see what we've got in this fancy leather satchel." The thief began pulling out books, his frown deepening. He unrolled Jacob's copy of the Fourth Scroll, then tossed it on the pile near Sarah's feet. "What's this?" He held up a vial of sacramental oil.

The bearded man reached into Sarah's burlap bag and groaned. "More books and baby clothes." He found the loaf of bread from Marta and tore off a huge chunk.

The other two thieves tussled over the rest of the loaf.

The balding man sniffed a jar of Jacob's incense. "What are you, a priest?"

"I'm a teacher," Jacob said through gritted teeth. "As you can see, I like to read."

"You think you're so smart?" His tormentor leaned over and backhanded Jacob across the face. "Well, traveling the river road on foot at this time of night was unwise, Teacher."

He rifled through Jacob's clothes at the bottom of his bag. "I bet you went to the funeral for that pompous high priest. It's about time someone stuck a knife in him."

Jacob was going to stick a knife in that loathsome criminal before the night was out.

The bearded man leafed through Sarah's treasured Book of Deborah. She let out a small gasp as he threw the red leather book on the pile in disgust. He narrowed his eyes at her. "What's that silver chain around your neck?"

She shook her head. "It's just a glass trinket."

"Give it to me." He held out a grimy hand.

She hesitated.

"It's all right," Jacob whispered.

She removed the chain with the teardrop amulet and handed it to the large man. He looked at it in the light, then shook his head and flung it on the pile. "A worthless piece of glass."

The sacrilege of these odious bandits eating the Bread of Life while their holy books and possessions were thrown around like garbage was galling.

"Have you two nothing of worth?" The balding man shook his club at them.

Jacob glanced at his wife, pregnant with the prophesied lord. After surviving demons and fortunetellers, he prayed to Patrimus their end wouldn't come from these menacing fools in the forest.

Lying on the open Book of Deborah, Sarah's glass pendant began to glow.

He looked at the passage at the bottom of the page fluttering in the breeze. *In due time, help comes from above to smite the wicked.*

He caught Sarah's eye. She noticed it too, but the thieves were oblivious.

"Nothing of worth to you anyway." Jacob risked a beating, but he needed to keep talking so Jonah could find them and hatch some sort of plan.

Where was he anyway? Jonah might be tempted to leave him, but surely he wouldn't abandon his sister.

She groaned and rubbed her forehead.

"What is it, miss?" asked the bearded man through a huge mouthful of bread.

Sarah lifted her ash-smudged face. "My back hurts, and I've hardly eaten today." She glanced at Jacob. "And I have a splitting headache that's getting worse by the minute."

A headache that's getting worse? Jonah must be near, hopefully seething with rage. Seeing his wife taken captive at this sordid encampment made Jacob's own blood boil.

"You need to let us go." He leaned forward, his legs tensed. "My wife's about to give birth any day."

"Seems like you're the one to blame for that, Teacher."

A dark shape rose on the boulder behind the two men. Sword in hand, Jonah crouched on the edge. As the balding man chuckled at his insult, Jonah leapt from ten feet off the ground and drove his blade through his shoulder and out beneath his ribcage, knocking his bearded partner to his knees. The balding man screeched and fell face first to the ground.

Jonah lay sprawled on the dirt behind them.

The bearded man picked up his knife and spun toward Jonah.

"Jonah, get up!" Jacob sprang to his feet, the hilt of Jonah's sword just two paces in front of him. But with his hands tied behind him, he was helpless to wield it.

Sarah lunged for the frying pan, scooped hot coals from the fire, and flung them at the bearded man's face.

He dropped the knife, howling with rage, and pawing at his face. Jacob charged him, shoulder first, and drove him into the rock. Jonah scrambled up with a large cook pot and slammed it into his head. The bearded man collapsed in a heap.

Sarah grabbed his knife then cut Jacob's bonds.

Shaking his wrists free from the rope, he took the knife and stepped in front of her. His eyes darted to the old man who stumbled backward into the horse's flank.

"Have mercy..." He held up his hands. "Have mercy on me, brother."

Jacob advanced on him, gripping the knife. "You don't deserve it, you despicable thief."

She laid her hand on his arm, trying to calm his pent-up rage.

"I'm all right," he said through heaving breaths.

The look in her green eyes told him she knew that was a lie. None of them were because one man lay dead at their feet and another injured and unconscious. Jacob badly wanted to kill the third.

Jonah wrenched his sword free from the bald man's corpse, awaiting their next move.

In his mind, Jacob could hear his father's voice. *Remember who you are.* He straightened his shoulders and shook the hair out of his eyes. He was a priest of the House of Eleazar, and he would not kill a man who had surrendered to them.

Besides, he had more pressing concerns, like the condition of his wife, who barely had the strength to stand.

Jacob dropped the knife and gathered her in his arms. "Are you hurt?"

"I don't think so."

He frowned at the red welt on her neck where the knife had pierced her skin. He brushed her neck with his fingertips, praying for healing for her wound and any other ill effects she or the baby may have suffered.

Sarah closed her eyes and breathed deeply, as if inhaling the prayer itself.

"What are we going to do about him?" Jonah eyed the trembling man as he wiped his sword off on a stranger's stolen shirt.

"We can't kill him, but I have another idea," Jacob said.

While Jonah guarded the old man and Sarah gathered their belongings, Jacob mixed an incense to make the thief sleep for at least eight hours and impair his memory.

Jonah pushed him to his knees while Jacob held his smoking censer under the man's wrinkled face. "We're taking the mare because I know you didn't come by her honestly."

The old man started to sway.

Jacob threw a ragged cloak over him as he succumbed to sleep. "By the time you wake up, we'll be long gone."

The bearded man received no such courtesy with his dose of sleeping incense.

Jacob turned to Sarah. "You can ride the horse up the mountain. When we get to the outcropping, we'll shelter there for the rest of the night."

She nodded, exhaustion and relief evident on her face.

Jonah sheathed his sword and stepped around the dead man face down in the dirt. He glanced at Sarah. "I had to do it."

"I know you did." She squeezed his shoulder. "Thank you."

Jacob nodded his gratitude also, but Jonah moved over to the horse and stroked its neck.

The glow from Sarah's necklace lit their path away from the grisly scene. Jonah followed behind them, talking softly to the speckled mare. Soon they emerged from the forest with the moon high in the sky and an abundance of stars overhead. The constellation of the Conquering Lion seemed to stand guard above the High Plain of Nirel.

"Do you hear that?" she whispered.

They stilled at the sound of hoofbeats approaching from the south.

Jonah wound the horse's reins over a low hanging branch at the edge of the forest. "I'm going to get closer to see if it's soldiers."

"At this time of night, who else would it be?" Jacob grabbed his arm. "You need to stay here."

Sarah cocked her head. "That might be a carriage."

Jonah shook his arm free. "We need to see who they are and if they stay on the river road or head up to the plateau where we plan to spend the night."

"You're right." Jacob had to admit that was sensible. They certainly didn't want to be taken by surprise again.

"Be careful," Sarah whispered as her brother ran in a low crouch toward the road.

A lantern bobbed on the front of a carriage as it rounded the bend.

"Get down," Jacob called.

Jonah hid behind a low thicket next to the road, his sword in his hand.

In the light of the nearly full moon, he'd have a good view of whoever was coming their way.

The carriage moved slowly down the deserted road.

Jacob turned to Sarah and whispered. "It seems like they're looking—"

The white center of her amulet swirled like a stoked flame. "Your necklace. It's getting brighter."

"Oh, no!" Sarah clenched her fist around the amulet, but white light seeped through her fingers. She pulled her cloak over it and the light burst through the gaps in her cloak, shining on her anguished face.

The driver of the carriage turned toward them.

Jonah sprang up. "Stop!" He waved his sword, chasing after it.

Jacob's heart hammered in his chest. "What is he doing?"

The carriage slowed to a stop as Jonah ran toward it.

"It's Grandmother and Seth!"

35

—————

THE DARK ROAD

Sarah clutched her necklace, that mysterious beacon of fire, and looked toward the heavens with a whispered *thank you*.

The carriage door opened, and Grandmother flew to Jonah and embraced him.

Sarah and Jacob hurried over to them as fast as she could manage.

"Oh, my dears. We were so worried." She kissed Sarah with tears in her eyes. "We saw the firestorm from the North Gate, and I knew you had to be near the canyon."

Sarah clung to her grandmother's slender shoulders. "It was like when you first brought me to the city, only worse." She glanced at the darkened plains to the west, reluctant to linger lest the evil one rediscovered them.

"We've got to go." Jacob motioned them toward the carriage. "There're bandits in the woods."

Jonah's hand jerked toward the hilt of his sword.

"Good heavens! You were set upon?" Grandmother's eyes darted between the three of them and landed on Jacob's swollen cheek. "Is anyone else hurt?"

"Just a few scratches and bruises, nothing Jacob couldn't handle." Sarah looked up at him, hoping that was true. But the full story would have to wait. The retelling would make her nauseous all over again.

Jonah broke away from their reunion. "I'll get the horse and scout the road ahead."

With a boost from Jacob, Sarah climbed into the carriage and sank onto the soft leather seat. Grandmother followed and sat across from her. The carriage springs groaned when Jacob ducked inside and joined them. His arm around her shoulders steadied her as the carriage rocked to a start.

After they got underway, she leaned her head on his dusty shoulder. "I really didn't want to give birth in a strange rock hideout."

Jacob pushed his bangs off his forehead. "Oh, I can't even think about that."

"I had to." She took his hand and placed it on her belly as it hardened again.

He sat up. "What?"

Grandmother leaned forward. "When did the contractions start?"

"An hour or two ago. At first, I wasn't sure given everything else going on and the effects on my stomach."

He winced. "Does it hurt?"

"Not really. It just feels weird." She yawned and snuggled closer to him.

"Just the beginning of the birth pangs then." Grandmother twisted her hands on her lap.

"How much longer until we get to the orphanage?" he asked.

"Four hours. Maybe more," Grandmother said.

Jacob tensed on the seat. "That long."

Jonah drew abreast of the carriage just then and reported

through the window that the road ahead was empty, and he would check behind them also.

As the road sloped upward to the High Plain of Nirel, Sarah's eyelids grew heavy. *Nirel*...Jacob once said it meant God's plowed field, that place where the faithful remnant gathered at the beginning of the age, drawn by the holy fire of Lord Uriel's staff that blazed in the darkness.

She reached inside her cloak and grasped the teardrop amulet that had led them out of their place of captivity. Her gaze dropped to her swollen belly. Soon the Heir to the Sacred Fire would pass through that same field, now overgrown and deserted.

"You both should try to get some sleep." Grandmother folded her hands. "We'll have a long night ahead of us."

SARAH JOLTED awake as the carriage hit a deep rut. Jacob slept beside her, his head tipped back and mouth half open. She rubbed her aching back. Grandmother smiled, bleary eyed and wrinkled on the seat opposite.

"What time is it?" Sarah whispered.

"I'd guess about three in the morning."

She looked out the window, but they must be under the tree canopy since there was little moonlight on the dark road. "Is Jonah all right?"

"Yes, the boy's stamina is something to behold."

It wasn't his stamina that had Sarah worried, but a private conversation with her brother would have to wait. For now, maybe he'd find a measure of solace alone with the mare and his scouting mission. "How much longer until we reach Amos and Elena?"

"A little over an hour would be my guess."

Sarah sucked in a breath as a contraction, stronger now,

arced across her abdomen. "My back hurts, and I so badly want to lie down."

Grandmother slid over and patted the seat next to her. Careful not to wake Jacob, Sarah scooted over to her. She lay on her side with her head on Grandmother's lap, and knees tucked to her chest as much as possible.

Grandmother rubbed her back, softly humming a lullaby. As tired as she was, Sarah knew that sleep would not come again until she was on the other side of giving birth.

Soon they turned onto the village road, and she was thankful for the slightly smoother ride. And yet, with each turn of the carriage wheels, she moved farther away from the holy city and the life she had dreamed of two years ago...and the far richer life she and Jacob had lived there.

"You'll have to go back soon."

Grandmother stroked her hair. "What, dear?"

"You'll need to return to the city soon."

"Yes, as soon as I know you and the baby are well. I don't want to raise suspicions by my absence. After all, we have work to do to clear Jacob's name."

"What?" He mumbled then repositioned himself and nodded off again.

Sarah feared clearing his name wouldn't be as easy as Grandmother made it sound. That her husband, who chose to spare the lives of their captors, would be accused of murdering his own father struck her as a grave injustice.

Jonah pulled abreast of the carriage to report that the road was clear all the way to the cart path to the old lodge. Grandmother sent him on ahead to wake Elena and Amos.

About twenty minutes later, they reached the old stone lodge, ablaze with light despite the pre-dawn hour.

Jacob and Grandmother helped her out of the carriage. Halfway to the front door, Sarah stumbled to a stop as a warm, wet liquid ran down her leg. Elena opened the door, and

Grandmother rushed to her, talking rapidly about Sarah's water breaking, labor progressing fast, and other things that Sarah couldn't grasp through the pain.

"I'll be in the barn with Seth and the horses." Jonah scurried away.

"Well, I didn't expect to see you again, Sarah." Elena pecked her cheek as they entered the house. "And you've been busy these past two years. A handsome husband and a baby coming very soon by the looks of things." She eyed Jacob. "You'd best get your wife upstairs."

"I'll be right behind you," Grandmother called from the kitchen where Amos was filling a basin with water.

Jacob put his arm around her and half carried her up the narrow staircase.

On the threshold of her former bedroom, her legs shook as another contraction squeezed her. A candle burned on the dresser, and Elena had piled towels and rags next to her old bed.

Sarah gripped his sleeve. "Stay with me."

"Of course. I didn't battle bandits and come all this way to hide out in the barn with your brother."

Two grueling hours later, Jacob knelt next to the bed and stared at his wife and son as he rested on her chest.

A hush had settled over the sparse bedroom after Elena departed, satisfied that Sarah didn't have any worrisome complications. In the holy stillness, Jacob thanked the living God for his courageous and compassionate wife and their newborn son...divine gifts of infinite worth.

If only his father and brother were here to behold the newest member of the House of Eleazar. But his father lay dead in the cold crypts, and his brother was left, blinded and alone, to hold off Jacob's accusers as long as possible.

"They're both doing so well, especially under such trying circumstances," Hannah whispered from the other side of the bed.

"Yes." Jacob brushed a lock of hair off Sarah's glistening forehead. "Maybe she didn't need me here after all."

"Oh, she needed you—as a husband not a healer, thankfully."

Sarah's eyes fluttered open. "I'll always need you...both of you."

The baby stirred at the sound of her voice.

Jacob leaned over and kissed his wife. "And I'll always be here..."

She smiled through her exhaustion. "Take him to the window, and show him the holy city."

Hannah picked up her swaddled grandson and placed him in Jacob's arms.

He held the tiny bundle and took shuffling steps to the south gable, fearful he might drop the Heir to the Sacred Fire on the short walk. He rested his cheek on the soft dark hair that curled at his ears.

As Jacob gently turned his son to look out the window, the baby blinked his brown eyes at him. There, in the distance, the holy city blazed like a white fire in the darkness before the dawn.

He forced down the lump in his throat. "So Elijah Eleazar, what do you think of the holy city...your city?"

The baby began to cry.

"I know," Jacob whispered as his own tears trickled down his bruised face.

A NOTE FROM THE AUTHOR

To learn more about the story world of *The Fourth Scroll* and the origin of the prophetess Deborah, join my monthly author newsletter. I'll send you a link to download the free short story *Eyes to See*, a prequel to The Sacred Fire Saga. Newsletter subscribers are always the first to receive my free short stories, publishing updates, and cover reveals. I also do fun giveaways throughout the year.

Download the free ebook at https://karengrunst.com/eyes-to-see.

If you enjoyed *The Fourth Scroll*, I'd be honored and grateful if you'd rate the book and leave a short review on your bookseller's website. Ratings and reviews help bring the story to the attention of other readers who value young adult fantasy with faith elements. Thank you so much!

ACKNOWLEDGMENTS

Writing a second book differs in significant ways from writing a debut novel. I'm now blessed with readers, so I couldn't take years to write the next book in the series. Also, I hoped to thrill those readers with a story that's even better than the preceding one.

But the tighter timeframe combined with self-doubt led to several bouts of fear and procrastination. Thank you, Jesus, for bringing me through the valleys of the creative process!

Author Amy Earls, you're the first person I go to for both pesky manuscript problems and book-marketing challenges. Thank you for being such a sweet friend and prayer partner. At some point, we must meet in person!

Every member of my enthusiastic team of beta readers brought a different focus, whether honing aspects of writing craft and pacing, evaluating spiritual content, or providing a teenager's perspective on the plot and characters. Amy Earls, Julie Hughes, Liz Johnson, Beth Mason, and Sarah Mason, I'm forever grateful for your insightful suggestions.

Bethany Kaczmarek, thank you so much for your excellent editorial advice and timely words of encouragement to spur me on to the finish line. I also appreciate your patience when I missed a few deadlines and submitted work to you at odd hours of the night.

Proofreader Erynn Newman, in addition to finding grammatical errors and typos, you went above and beyond by recommending helpful copy edits that clarified and tightened the manuscript.

Emilie Haney, many thanks for creating this book's striking cover. It's incredibly reassuring to know that the cover design for each installment in The Sacred Fire Saga is in such capable hands.

Annika Crum of A.C. Cartography, thank you for partnering with me to create the lovely map of Aclesia, a wonderful addition to the book and series. Your skills and attention to detail enhance the reader's experience of the story world.

Latin teacher Sarah Whipple, thank you for revising my amateur translations to make the Latin text accurate and authentic.

Family and friends, I appreciate you bearing with me while I wrestled with looming deadlines. You were gracious and supportive when I had to retreat to my study for long periods to write or revise.

Readers, thank you so much for taking a chance on a relatively new author! Your reviews, kind emails, and encouraging replies to my monthly newsletters are food for this writer's soul. May you find nourishment within the pages of *The Fourth Scroll*.

ABOUT THE AUTHOR

My love of epic fantasy series, especially those written from a Christian worldview, inspired me to write in the fantasy genre. Populating my stories are characters grappling with their fears and aspirations, doubts and faith. They, like us in the nonfictional world, are participants in a story much greater than they realize. *The Fourth Scroll* is the second book in The Sacred Fire Saga. To learn more about me and my young adult fantasy series, visit https://karengrunst.com.

facebook.com/karengrunst.author

instagram.com/karengrunst

goodreads.com/karengrunst